"Listen, what's the worst that can happen? You marry me, get your funding and in a few weeks toss me to the curb?"

"And what do you get out of this?"

Carter's smile was genuine. Strong. "You."

A whisper ran through her mind, carrying the thought that maybe he meant it. That maybe, as he'd said, he wanted her for more than restoring his reputation, saving his company. That he cared. Maybe even loved her. But that thought was too scary, too improbable, so she pushed it aside. "Carter, we should be smart about this."

"I'm done being smart, Daphne," he answered. "Maybe I never acted smart to begin with. All I know is that I want to marry you. I want to leap off that bridge and not worry about what's waiting below." He caught her hand, running his touch along her finger. "Do something unexpected, Daphne. Marry me."

"Something unexpected," she echoed, her gaze meeting his. Earnest truth shone in his eyes, and something within Daphne latched on to that, believing he was different. Believing that this could work. "Yes, I'll marry you."

P9-DMJ-405

Dear Reader,

Readers often ask me how much of my books are drawn from my own life. The answer varies—sometimes a lot, sometimes a little. Ideas spring from a wide variety of places—things I read, things I do, things I see. When one book is done, I'm anxious to start the next, to take another idea and see how it works on paper.

I am a huge fan of coffee shops, and in fact wrote most of the pages you see here in coffee shops while sipping an iced latte and (unsuccessfully) trying to avoid the cookie temptations. And several years ago my husband bought his own business—an experience which gave me lots of ideas when it came to writing about Carter's company, in *Married by Morning.*

My own twentieth class reunion is this year, which inspired the idea behind *Back to Mr & Mrs.* It's been a year of looking over the past, of seeing how I've changed—and how I haven't—since those high school years. I still have the same best friend I always had, though we live far apart these days and only get to catch up in person once a year. And I still feel twenty-one, even if my driver's license tells me otherwise.

So, pour yourself a cup of Java coffee, curl up in a cushy chair and enjoy this MAKEOVER BRIDE & GROOM duet. As for me, I'm getting to work on another book—with a little caffeine fuel along for the ride!

Shirley

SHIRLEY JUMP
Married by Morning

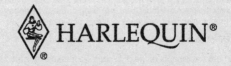

HARLEQUIN®

TORONTO • NEW YORK • LONDON
AMSTERDAM • PARIS • SYDNEY • HAMBURG
STOCKHOLM • ATHENS • TOKYO • MILAN • MADRID
PRAGUE • WARSAW • BUDAPEST • AUCKLAND

ISBN-13: 978-0-373-18304-3
ISBN-10:   0-373-18304-6

MARRIED BY MORNING

First North American Publication 2007.

www.eHarlequin.com

Printed in U.S.A.

Sugar and Spice, the anthology that featured Shirley Jump's novella "Twelve Days," recently hit the *New York Times, USA TODAY* and *Publishers Weekly* bestseller lists.

Though she's thrilled to see her books in stores around the world, Shirley mostly writes because it gives her an excuse to avoid cleaning the toilets and helps feed her shoe habit.

To learn more, visit her Web site at www.shirleyjump.com.

A word of dating advice from Shirley Jump:
"Forget those quizzes in women's magazines. The best way to determine if this man is the one is to break out the board games. If he restrains his inner titan during *Monopoly,* doesn't chortle in glee at world domination during *Risk* and is nonplussed by the addition of two sets of twins in *The Game of Life,* then he's worth taking to the next level in Love."

For my children, who have added a dimension of fun to my life that I never expected. Having them has taught me that it's okay to completely humiliate yourself in a driveway basketball game and that the point of Scrabble isn't to win or show off my vocabulary skills, but to share laughs and groans with the family.

I love you both, more and more every day. Every laugh, every smile and especially every hug is a treasure I hold dear to my heart.

CHAPTER ONE

CARTER MATTHEWS screamed into the parking lot, road gravel spitting a wake behind him as he slid his red Lexus into a front space. The ads had said the car could go zero to sixty in the blink of an eye. They had lied.

Carter's new toy could go zero to a *hundred,* making the Lexus worth every penny.

He slid out of the car, feeling a twinge of guilt that he'd blown off most of the workday to take the car out for a spin. Pearl, his assistant, had given him her famous evil eye as he'd darted out the door this morning, barely five minutes after striding through it. What Pearl didn't understand was that TweedleDee Toys was undoubtedly better off when Carter wasn't running the ship.

"Mr. Matthews! I'm glad I found you!"

He spun around. Mike, TweedleDee's

design intern, scrambled across the parking lot, trying to hold a bulky paper bag against his chest with one hand while keeping his glasses on his nose with the other. "I…well, we, had this brainstorm today and the guys wanted me to rush over to you." He thrust the bag at Carter, then caught his breath. "Meet Cemetery Kitty. We think it's going to revolutionize the stuffed animal industry."

"Cemetery Kitty? As in another stuffed animal?" Carter tried to work some enthusiasm into his voice. This week, he'd given his toy designers a single task—to come up with something to wow the buyers at this fall's Toy Convention. He'd expected a water blasting outdoor gun, a snazzy remote control car, anything but one more faux fur pet.

"Are you going to look at it now?" Mike's entire body went frenetic with anticipation. He clasped and unclasped his hands, nodding at the bag. "You, ah, haven't been in the office all that much, so I thought I'd track you down. If you like it, we can rush right into production."

The stuffed toy would undoubtedly be one more in a string of failures, but he didn't voice his reservations, not while he was still riding the high of driving his new car. He had no desire to ruin that by inserting the failing toy business into the mix.

"It's been a long day. I'll look at it later. But thanks." He gave Mike a wave, then headed into his building.

The intern who had enthusiastically cleaned out the office supplies cupboard and color-coded the Post-it notes, remained undaunted and caught up with Carter. "Mr. Matthews?"

Carter turned around, at the same time tapping the car's locking remote, waiting for the answering beep. "Yeah, Mike?"

"Uh, the guys are kinda concerned," Mike said, clearly here as the sacrificial lamb for the employees. "You're not at work a whole lot and well, with your uncle Harry gone and all, we, ah, kind of wanted some direction."

Carter glanced at the Lexus. About the only thing he had experience directing was a fast car. And a few fast women. Every time he tried to manage the toy company, all he'd done was manage it further underground.

So he'd abandoned it today, just as he had last Wednesday to play golf, and the Tuesday before that for a rousing tennis match with his brother. Lately he'd been out of the office more than in. Considering Carter's managerial abilities, it was a good thing all around if he stayed away.

And yet, he couldn't bring himself to hire a manager. To admit failure.

Again.

"I'll see you tomorrow, Mike," Carter said, because he didn't have an answer to the whole direction thing. Hell, even Carter didn't know which direction to head.

Mike hesitated a second longer, then pushed his glasses up his nose and said goodbye. He crossed the lot, shoulders hunched, steps heavy and measured and looked back, two, three times, then slipped into his battered ten-year-old green truck and left.

Carter let out a sigh, climbed the stairs to his apartment, let himself in, dropped his keys in the crystal dish by the door, then opened the bag.

Inside was a cat. Life-size, gray and white striped fur, looking reasonably realistic. Certainly not the blockbuster he'd been expecting, given Mike's raving.

But pretty much par for the course at TweedleDee Toys.

He flicked the on/off switch. The furry thing rolled over, thrust its four paws into the air and let out a plaintive belching squeak. The cat shivered twice and went still.

"Just what a toy company needs," Carter muttered. "A cat that plays dead."

He tossed the play animal into a chair and crossed to his tidy, stainless steel kitchen. After this, he needed a stiff drink, a pretty woman and a long vacation, preferably on some desert island.

But his liquor cabinet was empty, his apartment devoid of anything female since Cecilia had walked out in a huff last Tuesday and his vocabulary had been missing the words "extended vacation" since he'd taken over the top spot at TweedleDee Toys.

A mistake of epic proportions.

He had no idea what his uncle Harry had been thinking when he'd written his will and left Carter in charge of a toy company. If anything, his twin brother Cade would have been a more logical choice. Cade, the organized one, the one who could take on a project and see it through to the finish line. He'd done that at their father's law firm and now, after leaving there, was working with his wife, Melanie, building her Cuppa Life coffee shop franchise throughout the Midwest.

Unlike Carter, whose greatest accomplishment in life had been running Uncle Harry's company into the ground.

Not to mention, disappointing his father. In his nearly forty years of life, Carter had managed to do only one thing well—perfect the art of being a disappointment.

He glanced around the apartment he'd moved into last month, to be closer to TweedleDee Toys and to escape the constant disapproval of his father back in Indianapolis. The space was neat, tidy and perfect—and totally devoid of personality. It didn't welcome or invite him in at the end of the day. The apartment simply existed, like something out of a catalog.

The Pier 1 furniture, the pale beige walls, all chosen by a decorator because Carter hadn't had the time or inclination. A weekly maid service polished the glass coffee table and set it at a right angle with the lines in the area rug.

Every space he'd ever lived in had been like this. Cold, impersonal and cared for by someone else. Just as he had been most of his life. He'd never settled down, never found his calling, and hadn't wanted to until the reading of Uncle Harry's will.

Six months ago, Uncle Harry's boat, *The Jokester,* had been found drifting at sea somewhere in the Atlantic. The Coast Guard had searched, then finally declared him dead two months ago, an announcement that seemed to make Carter's father, Jonathon, Harry's only brother, even more withdrawn and colder than usual.

At the reading of the will, Carter had looked around at his family—Cade and his father—and realized each of them had a purpose. Cade had Melanie, the franchise. Jonathon had the law practice. They seemed to be holding a card that Carter had never seen.

And then, when the stunning news that Uncle Harry had left TweedleDee Toys to Carter came out, the crazy thought that

Carter could *be* something had popped up. The attorney had handed over the ownership of TweedleDee Toys and Carter's father had let out a snort of derision. "You'll be filing bankruptcy in a month. That place was a mess when my brother ran it and it's undoubtedly only gotten worse in his absence."

A thousand times before his father had predicted Carter's failure—with pinpoint accuracy. For some reason, though, that day the comment had gotten Carter's dander up. "Never," Carter said to his father. "I can turn that company around."

His father had laughed, then shook his head. "Face it, Carter. You're not made of CEO material."

The only thing that had kept Carter from throwing in the towel in the last two months was the knowledge that he would once again prove his father right. And if there was one thing Carter was tired of doing, it was that.

Their father was a perfectionist. Every detail of his life was organized and filed, structured and meticulous. He expected nothing less of his sons. Cade, who had followed him into the family law practice, had measured up to that impossible standard while Carter had continually fell at least a mile short.

Carter shrugged off the thoughts, then crossed to the kitchen and opened the fridge, found a few sips of red wine left in a bottle shoved behind the expired carton of milk and poured the alcohol into a glass. "Cheers," he said, hoisting the drink toward the stiff furball in his armchair. "I think you've got the better end of the deal, my petrified friend."

He had just tipped the glass into his mouth when someone started banging at his door. Nosy Mrs. Beedleman and her binoculars, he was sure, had seen him and Cemetery Kitty through her courtyard window. And, as Mrs. Beedleman was wont to do, had assumed the worst about him and called the authorities.

Again.

Carter sighed, placed the glass on the counter and opened his apartment door.

"Let me guess," he said to the slim brunette in his hall. She wore a funky pair of dark purple glasses that turned up at the corners, in that popular sixties style. Tall, thin, she wore her brown hair in an angle cut bob that set off a graceful neck. But the suit she had on was all business and Carter knew better than to flirt with a government employee. "You're from the ASPCA and you're here to write me up on charges of animal cruelty, right?"

"No. I—"

"The thing is stuffed. Tomorrow, I'm firing the guys who invented it. So go on back to the office or wherever you came from because there's no dead cat in my apartment. At least, not a real one."

She blinked. "Dead cat?"

"I told you, it's not real. It's the Cemetery Kitty toy."

She blanched. "Uh, I think I knocked on the wrong door. Thanks anyway." The woman turned to leave.

She looked like someone he knew, but hell, so did half the city of Lawford. As a new CEO, he made more friends he didn't need at city networking events and golf tourneys, then forgot their names as soon as he put on his coat.

Still, something was familiar about this

woman. Not familiar in the kind of way that told him he'd dated her, though.

Had he?

How deplorable. He had dated so many women, he'd forgotten more than he remembered. Unlike Cade, who had found his true love in high school, married her after graduation and was still enjoying the fairy tale.

Carter was more of the big, bad wolf smart fathers warned their daughters about rather than the prince on the white horse.

The woman in his hallway had a long, delicate face with a slim nose and defined cheekbones, giving her a Grace Kelly kind of beauty. But unlike the screen legend, her hair was a medium brown, and the easy way it skipped over her jawline and neck seemed made for convertibles and lazy summer days. And her legs—well, hell, they were made for a lot of things he was pretty sure were illegal in Indiana.

Whoa. He needed a bigger drink.

Either way, hers was the first friendly face he'd seen all day. And here he was chasing her from his apartment, like a fool. "Wait."

She pivoted away from the elevator. "Can we start over?"

She paused a moment, then relented and returned to his doorway.

He ran a hand over his face. "Sorry. It's been a long day. I've got an unmarketable stuffed cat sitting on my recliner and I'm out of wine. Let me try this again. I'm Carter Matthews, and you are?"

"Daphne Williams."

Daphne. Didn't ring any bells.

"It's a pleasure to meet you, Daphne." He slipped on the smile that had won a number of women's hearts—and broken a few, too. "What brings you by?"

"I have a message for you."

"Now that's intriguing." Carter leaned against the door frame and sent a second glance running over her. "And what might that be?"

She smiled, any trace of friendliness gone. "Actually, a little hate mail."

He thought of telling her where she could stick her hate mail, then reconsidered.

She was, after all, a pretty woman and he had wished for one a few minutes earlier. He had the drink, albeit a thimbleful a wine, and with the certain demise of TweedleDee Toys now that his designers had launched a goth theme for spring, he'd have that vacation he wanted—a permanent one.

Be careful what you wish for, Matthews. It might just come true in spades.

Yet again, he was proving his father's adage that he was about as useful as snow in August. Carter hated when his father was right—and hated how easy it had become to be the kind of man who fell instead of rose to the occasion.

"Tell me who hates me now," Carter said. Besides his entire staff, and himself, of course.

"Me."

"You? Why?" Oh Lord, she *must* be an ex-girlfriend. Definitely a sign he was dating and drinking too much.

Daphne Williams parked a fist on her hip and glared at him. "You made me break up with my boyfriend for no good reason."

"Are you insane? I don't even know you."

"No, but you do know a—" she reached in her pocket and pulled out a small card

"—Cecilia, who sent you a breakup basket today."

Oh, damn. That really did take the cake for his day.

"A breakup basket?" Not that he hadn't been more or less expecting something similar from Cecilia, who had made it clear that his inability to commit was no way to conduct a relationship.

Cecilia had expected the usual Carter Matthews treatment—dinner at fancy restaurants, drinks in jazz bars, impromptu trips to a B&B, but when Carter had told her he needed to spend his time making a stab at this CEO instead of stealing away with her for weekend rendezvous and late nights on the dance floor, she'd thrown a fit.

"According to Cecilia," Daphne went on, "you're a no-good jerk and she doesn't want to see your face ever again, even if you were—" for this, she looked down at the card for the exact wording "—the last cockroach left on earth."

"Ouch."

"And this, I believe, is yours, not mine." She pivoted, picked up a massive black wicker basket he hadn't noticed earlier and thrust the thing into his arms. Skulls and crossbones decorated the outside, along with words like "never again" and "make hate, not love".

Inside the basket were all kinds of goodies. A voodoo doll with spiky dark hair that he suspected was supposed to be him. Stuffed and tortured with pins and red X's marking the mortal wounds. A half-dozen dead, shriveled black roses, a copy of *Men Who Are Jerks and The Women Who Dump Them*, a can of dog food with a spoon taped to the side, and a pint-size bottle of Lester Jester's Eau de Skunk.

"Guess she wanted to get her message across," he said.

"You must be one heck of a boyfriend."

"I'm actually a very nice guy."

She arched a brow at him. Apparently it was too late to make a good first impression.

Carter glanced again at the voodoo doll and noticed the hat pins sticking out of its eyeballs. Granted, that didn't speak well for him. "I don't get it. Tell me how *my* breakup ruined *your* life."

"This—" she pointed at the basket "—was delivered to me."

"I'll be sure to complain to the delivery company."

"Too late. I already ended a perfectly good relationship because of this thing."

"Did it breed in your living room? Or were you totally overcome by the fumes of Lester's skunk aroma?"

"I thought it was from *my* boyfriend." She glared at him as if every glitch in the universe was Carter's fault. A few he'd lay claim to, but not this one. "So I broke up with him."

He smirked. "A preemptive strike?"

She colored. Clearly Daphne Williams didn't like having the tables turned on her. "Yes."

"Didn't you read the card?"

"I didn't open the box until…after."

He tried to bite back his laughter but gave up the effort. "You broke up with your boyfriend, thinking he was breaking up with you, and you hadn't even opened the box?"

She parked her fists on her trim little hips. "I have had a very bad day."

"Well, so have I." He grinned. "But you

just made me laugh, so it's starting to improve."

She gave him a glare. "I don't find this funny."

He raised the can of liver-flavored dog food in her direction. "I can't believe you ruined a relationship over this."

"It's your fault."

"It is not."

"If you hadn't been such a horrible boyfriend, Cecilia wouldn't have sent you this and I wouldn't have thought it was meant for me and ended things with Jerry." She threw up her hands. "You have no idea how this throws a wrench into all my plans. I needed Jerry, and not just for a little dim sum on Friday nights."

He shook his head, needing a second to follow her long-winded logic. He hadn't had any dinner and the lack of sustenance had his brain firing in the wrong directions. "First off, I wasn't a horrible boyfriend." He thought a second. "Well, I wasn't *exactly* a horrible boyfriend. Second, you breaking up with Jerry was your choice, not mine. So I don't see why I owe you anything at all."

"I truly don't care what you think, Mr. Matthews. The way I see it, you owe me a favor. Two, in fact, because I lugged this thing all the way up to the fourth floor to deliver it to the right recipient."

"I disagree. I say Jerry was just waiting for an excuse to break up. My basket happened to be handy. So there's no favor required here at all." He started to shut his door.

She blocked him with a dark blue two-inch heel. "That's not true. I was a wonderful girlfriend."

He gave her a sardonic grin. "If you were so wonderful, then why did he let you get away so easily?"

Carter Matthews looked at Daphne Williams's furious, silent face and thought he'd never seen anything so pretty as a woman who didn't have a ready retort. She stepped back, sputtering and steaming, but not a single word came out.

"Have a good day, Miss Williams," he said, and shut his door.

Then he realized winning the battle didn't seem quite so victorious, considering he was left alone with a faux dead cat and a basket full of hate messages.

And a few truths about himself that weren't so fun to face.

Daphne stomped her way back to her apartment, considering various methods of torturing and killing Carter Matthews. She rejected drawing and quartering as too kind.

The man had the gall to make an analysis of her life when he was the one being sent a pin-stuffed voodoo doll? She'd been a darn good girlfriend to Jerry, even putting up with his endless obsession with Mortal Kombat, figuring the man had a dream and she should support him as he supported her.

Well, he didn't exactly support her. Or understand what she did. Or listen to eighty percent of what she said, because he called her work as a creativity coach "way above his mental ability level."

That part might have been true.

In the beginning, Daphne had found him distracted, and endearing. Then, in the last few weeks, his inattentiveness had become annoying.

Hurtful.

But he had been behind her idea of building a creativity center for children. It was the one thing that drove Daphne, fueled her desire to create all that she had never had as a child. A center like that could be a place of mental freedom, allowing kids to open their imaginations to the world.

To have fun, to create. And maybe, to feel like their ideas, their creations, were welcomed.

Jerry, the indulged only child of wealthy parents, had pledged to give her the start-up funds, then continue his support through the family foundation. Groundbreaking was scheduled to happen in two weeks—

Or had been anyway.

She'd had her funding and a comfortable relationship that demanded nearly nothing of her, until she'd made that rash—

Preemptive strike.

Whatever. She refused to use Carter Matthews's words, even if her mind might betray her.

Her doorbell rang and Daphne crossed to it, half hoping Jerry would be there, ball cap in hand, calling the whole thing a silly mix-up. And half hoping he wasn't.

Maybe the Breakup Basket had been a sign—or an open door—to force Daphne to change her life. To do more than go to work and come home to an empty apartment and an empty heart.

She shook off the thought as she opened the door. All she needed was a minute to recoup and get her plans back on track.

"How was Reno?" Kim, her best friend from kindergarten on up, stood on the other side of the door, a steaming bag from Garden Palace Chinese in one hand and a bottle of Jose Cuervo ready-mixed margaritas in the other.

There were many reasons why Kim was her best friend. And she was holding two of them.

Daphne opened the door wider, waving Kim in and relieving her of her burden. "The creativity convention in Reno was fine. It was the trip home that stunk. My direct flight was delayed—twice—then forced to land in Sioux City when the pilot's appendix burst. They lost my luggage somewhere over the continental United States, I lost my lunch in

the turbo-jet's bathroom during ungodly tur-
bulence and then finally lost my car."

"Your car?"

Daphne nodded. "I forgot where I parked
it in the Indianapolis lot. Even the guy who
ran the lot couldn't find it. So he gave me a
phone number and told me to call the
manager after nine tomorrow."

"Wow, talk about a bad day."

"I came home to worse." Daphne sighed,
grabbing some dishes, then sinking into a
chair at her kitchen table and telling Kim
about the basket, her mistaken call to Jerry,
and the mix-up with Carter Matthews. "That
man is an evil monster, Kim. We should hang
a warning poster about him outside the
building."

Kim laughed, her blond ponytail swinging and her bright green eyes dancing as
she did. "Aw, he's not that bad. He's the guy
who just moved into 4-B right?" Daphne
nodded. "The women around here have
been buzzing about our new neighbor and
trying to outdo each other to snag one of the
last bachelors standing."

"Why?"

"Don't you read the paper? He's a frequent flyer in Gloria's Gossip and Gab column. You know, one of those moderately wealthy, handsome guys who think marriage is for wimps. If that's what evil monsters look like, sign me up for the movie."

Daphne thought of Carter Matthews's dark brown hair, the way the waves were displaced when he ran his fingers through it, leaving him looking like he just tumbled out of bed. His eyes, deep and blue, the kind most women fantasized about. *Most* women, though. Not her. And not Cecilia anymore, either, apparently. "Looks can't make up for bad personality."

"But they sure help." Kim winked. "So, what are you going to do about Jerry?"

Daphne sighed. "Honestly, I'm relieved. Jerry wasn't exactly Prince Charming."

"Then why did you stay with him for five months?"

She shrugged. "I guess I thought he had all the qualities I wanted, or maybe did, somewhere in there. He was like a houseplant—a little time and some sunlight and he'd grow into what I needed."

Kim laughed. "That man needed way more than a little fertilizer."

"You're right." Daphne poured them each a margarita, then took a couple sips of her own before going on. The tequila hit her brain fast, skipping right past her empty stomach. "He was just so supportive of the creativity center, I thought—"

"You could turn ground chuck into sirloin?"

Daphne laughed. "I'll never tell Carter Matthews this, but he did me a favor. It was time to break up with Jerry. I just wish the creativity center didn't have to be part of it, too."

"You don't think he'll look past this and still put his money into it, out of a sense of civic duty or something?"

"Nope. He made that really clear." Daphne dished up some Chinese food for each of them, then toyed with a fortune cookie. "Do you know what I really want, Kim?"

"Besides hitting the lottery?"

"A man who cares about me. About what's important to me. Someone who…" She paused a minute. "I don't know, fills in the gaps."

"Are we replaying the dialogue from a Tom Cruise movie?"

Daphne laughed again. "No. I guess it's more that I want to have fun, but I never seem to do it. I go to work, I come home and I live the same day three hundred and sixty-five days a year."

"Something you've been doing for a long time," Kim said with the soft tones of a longtime friend.

"Yeah." Daphne shook off the thoughts. "Anyway, I've just had a heck of a day. Makes me all melancholy. I think once I find a new supporter for the creativity center, I'll feel better."

Kim's hand covered hers. "Don't worry, Ducky, you'll think of something," she said, lapsing into Daphne's childhood nickname. When she'd been a child, it had started out as the second half of Daffy Duck, a tease from kids who paired her first name with the cartoon character. As she'd gotten older, the Ducky part had stuck, because, as Kim said, Daphne had this uncanny ability to bounce back from anything and always ride above a disaster. She'd turned companies around with her creativity training and usually managed to keep a sunny perspective on life.

Until Carter Matthews had ruined everything.

Now the duck was starting to sink. Well, she wasn't going under without taking someone else along for a well-deserved drowning, too.

CHAPTER TWO

ON WEDNESDAY morning, Carter had resolved to make things better, to once again try on that CEO hat. Maybe even take a step forward from yesterday's disaster.

He hadn't. If anything, he'd made things worse.

Before he'd left his apartment, his best toy designer had called, irate that Carter had rejected Cemetery Kitty. The toy designer had pitched a tantrum of epic proportions, saying he was quitting and in the process, gave Carter an angry, rambling speech about working with idiots and a corporate culture worthy of sewer workers.

That had stung. Sewer workers were probably more creative than his team, damn it. At least they unplugged problems, instead of creating them.

The call had put him behind schedule, and if there was one thing Carter didn't want, it was a disruption in his schedule. His new, as of today, highly responsible schedule.

He was going to make this thing work— even if it took getting to the office at the crack of dawn and staying till ten—*p.m.*, instead of his usual ten a.m. quitting time.

This morning, he'd hoped to be in the parking garage at seven-nineteen in the morning, in his office by seven-thirty. He glanced at his watch. Eight-oh-seven.

Great. Just what he needed. To be late and one toy designer short.

This CEO business had turned out to be far more time consuming than Carter had expected. It wasn't about the missed golf games, the canceled dates, or his forgetfulness to restock his fridge. It was the way the business seemed to consume his every thought, haunting him even when he wasn't there. Now he understood why his twin brother's work life had nearly cost him his marriage.

Cade had seen the light, however, and exited the law work he hated in favor of supporting Melanie's business. Now Cade was home with

Melanie every night, rekindling the flame that had nearly gone out in their marriage.

Somewhere along the way, Carter had gotten the idea that he could prove himself as a responsible person, too. Considering how TweedleDee Toys was going, all he was proving was his ability to fail.

He'd avoided the office all these weeks because of the certain knowledge that despite his best intentions, he didn't have what it took to rescue the company. Every attempt he made to improve—reduce the bottom line, increase production, shore up morale—had been met with resistance by employees too used to being on their own—

And far too familiar with Carter's indulgent past.

Carter pushed the thoughts away and stepped out of the building and into the bright, warm sunshine. Daphne Williams stood in the parking lot, her keys in one hand, cell phone in the other, and an exasperated expression on her face. "What do you mean, you towed it? I didn't see a No Parking sign when I left it in the long-term lot." A pause. "That wasn't the long-term lot? Since when?" Another pause. "If you're going to completely reconfigure the airport parking lot, you could at least put up a sign. Mail out a flyer. Let people know so they don't—" She let out a huff at being interrupted. "Of course. I'll be sure to fill out the comment card on my next visit to the airport. You can count on that." Then she clicked the phone shut and let out a half-scream/half-groan of frustration.

"Having a good day?" he asked, teasing her. Because he couldn't resist and because, hell, he was already late.

She wheeled on him. "If you must ask, and I can tell by the glint in your eyes that you must, no, I'm not." Her voice broke on the last words and for a moment, he felt awful. "I have to be at a meeting in twenty minutes and my car isn't where it's supposed to be, and the place that towed it isn't open until ten." She drew in a breath, seemed to steady herself, then her face brightened. "Well, I always did enjoy the adventure of a cab ride before breakfast." Daphne flipped out her phone and started to scroll through the programmed numbers, muttering to herself as she did. "What was the name of that taxi company?"

Guilt came in many forms, Carter realized. Some of them brunette and slim and with a crushed, vulnerable look in wide chocolate eyes. "Where's your meeting?"

"Seventh and Vine."

"My office is on Eighth. Let me give you a ride."

She glanced up from the phone. "Why?"

"It's the neighborly thing to do."

"Well, Mr. Matthews, last I checked, you weren't feeling too neighborly toward me. If I remember right, you called me insane and shut your door in my face."

"Not one of my finer moments." Heck, he hadn't had many of those at all. But today, Carter Matthews was turning over a new leaf.

Again.

She ran a hand through her hair, displacing the brunette tendrils. They settled around her neck with little flips at the ends. On another woman, he might have found that attractive.

Hell, who was he kidding? He *did* find it attractive, especially on Daphne Williams.

With the way she had her hips parked to one side and her wide brown eyes giving him that perpetual look of frustration, he knew he got to her, too.

Granted, probably not in the same gut-stirring, fire-igniting, hormone-lighting manner, but at least she wasn't immune to his charms.

Daphne sighed. "Yesterday wasn't one of my finer moments, either," she said. "And I would appreciate the ride. Besides, you owe me."

"I do at that," he said, in a voice several octaves deeper than he'd intended. He cleared his throat, ridding it of the damnable frog inside, and pressed on the long metal handle of the glass door that led to the parking garage, holding it open for her to pass through.

And wondering if he'd just made a huge mistake.

When Daphne had agreed to ride with Carter Matthews, she hadn't thought about the consequences of squeezing into his little red two-door sports car. It was a hardtop convertible, exactly what she'd expected from Indiana's most notorious bachelor.

But what was worse about the Lexus was its size. The car had all the room of a takeout box and made her overwhelmingly more aware of what Kim had called his more attractive assets.

Okay, he *was* cute. Another woman might like the way his hair waved at the top, one lock falling down on his forehead from time to time. Another woman might like the deep dark blue of his eyes, the way they seemed to reflect everything he looked at, especially her own image, as if he were a human mirror.

And especially the way he set her off-kilter—the one feeling Daphne had done a darn good job of avoiding.

Until Carter Matthews came along.

"I know, the car's a stereotype," he said, reading her mind as he put the powerful vehicle into gear. A growl erupted from the engine, as if the Lexus wanted to show Daphne a little speed.

"It does scream bachelor," she replied. "And from what the news has said about you, you're the kind of guy who's only capable of an intimate relationship with your steering wheel."

He laughed at that. "Gloria does get a few good lines in her gossip column from time to time. The woman can turn a phrase, even if her observations are a bit...skewed." Carter took a left on Prince Street, causing Daphne to sway a little toward his side. Her arm brushed against his, and she jerked it back. "Was the all-perfect, now-departed-from-your-life Jerry a car nut?"

Daphne laughed. "Definitely not. Jerry didn't even like to drive. He preferred to let me be behind the wheel."

"Whoa. What a man."

Daphne let out a chuff. She refused to give Carter the satisfaction of knowing she was happy Jerry was out of her life. "You don't have to drive the girl around to be a man."

"Whatever happened to chivalry? Taking care of your woman and all that?" He braked for a stoplight, drumming his fingers on the top of the leather-wrapped steering wheel, clearly annoyed by the wait. His dark blue suit jacket strained against his shoulders.

"For your information, I don't need

anyone to take care of me. I'm perfectly capable of taking care of myself."

"Oh. You're one of *those* women."

"What do you mean, one of those women?"

"The kind who says she doesn't need a man when all she really needs is to meet the *right* man."

Daphne shook her head. "I should have expected a line like that out of someone like you."

"I see my reputation has preceded me once again." He tossed her a grin, then returned his attention to the road. "Just don't believe everything you read." A sliver of something vulnerable slipped in between his words, but disappeared just as quickly.

She must have imagined it, Daphne decided.

This was exactly why she'd slipped into that rut with Jerry. To avoid men who pushed her buttons, who drove her crazy. An unpredictable, frustrating man like Carter Matthews should come with a Do Not Disturb sign.

Especially when that lock of hair fell down across his forehead again and everything within her itched to brush it back. It had to be the car. Something about a convertible made her want to do crazy things.

Things that pulled her focus away from what was important—work, not relationships. Work provided the steady concrete base Daphne needed in her life. People might let her down, but her job never did.

The light changed to green. The sound of the accelerator giving the car more gas sounded suspiciously like Carter saying, "Uh-huh."

"So, what do you do?" Daphne asked, not to get to know Carter better, but only to change the subject toward anything other than male driving habits and how they could be relationship portents.

"When I'm not starring in the pages of the paper?"

She nodded.

"I own TweedleDee Toys." He let out a heavy sigh and slowed as they approached orange signs denoting an ongoing construction project, flicking a glance at his watch as he did. She noticed the interior of his car was as neat as his apartment had been. Not a speck of dust or so much as a lone French fry littered any of the surfaces. New car smell hung sweet and heavy in the air. "Or at least I do today. The way things have been going, I might not tomorrow."

She shouldn't ask. She shouldn't care. But the little part of her that always did her job *did* care. And felt that surge of need to help.

This time, it was a masochistic urge, she thought as Carter circumvented some roadwork by zipping down Central and back up Washington to Third. It had to have been the lines in his face, the ones that seemed to say he'd been having a hell of a last few weeks. "What do you mean, you might not have the company anymore soon?"

"I think you've had enough bad news for a couple days. I won't burden you with mine." He turned and grinned again, this time a softer, easier, more friendly smile.

In some countries it might even be considered cute.

The masochistic urge to help him multiplied tenfold. Okay, he had a nice smile. Too bad he was an arrogant jerk who drove women away and ruined other people's love lives.

They ran into the same construction again at the end of Third Street. She saw him check his watch a second time, clearly not happy with the delay.

They sat there, idling in stopped traffic. She glanced at Carter and softened. Maybe her heart was bleeding a little this morning. Maybe she was overtired, or underfed. Either way, she sat there and began to think a guy with a smile like that couldn't be all bad. Could he?

"I'm a corporate creativity coach," she said. From all that she'd read about Carter Matthews in the local papers, he was new to the CEO thing and could likely use a little help.

Okay, maybe a lot.

"Are you the one who made toilet paper fun?"

She laughed. "That's probably not the best job on my résumé—"

"But it is the cleanest." He gave her a teasing grin. "What a small world. Your company has been on my To Do list for weeks. I even looked it up on the Internet, which is why you looked so familiar last night. Your firm came highly recommended by my brother."

Heat rose in her cheeks at the unexpected praise. "Thanks. We've had some nice success in the last couple of years."

He gestured toward the stopped cars in front of them. "If I had to be stuck in traffic with anyone, I'm glad it's you. Creativity is the one thing my company—and my employees—seem to be lacking."

"But you're a toy company. Isn't fun supposed to be part of your company motto?"

He inched the car forward. "You might want to tell my staff that, considering our latest creation was Cemetery Kitty. 'Come watch her roll over and play dead.'"

"Oh, my." Daphne put a hand over her mouth, holding back a laugh. "That's bad. That's really bad."

"I can practically hear the whoosh of my corporate profits going down the white porcelain river ride."

"What you need is a little creativity boost for your team."

"What I need is a miracle," he muttered,

and once again the shade in his eyes drew back enough for her to see he was worried.

Another wave of sympathy ran through Daphne. She understood what that was like. In the early days at Creativity Masters, she had faced those uphill battles alone because she hadn't been able to afford help. She'd had to prove she could make a living at something as "silly" as creativity. And she had, in spades.

A construction worker in an orange vest waved them forward. Carter, following the cars before him, wove his way between the bright neon cones and warning signs. The Lexus bumped a little over the rough road, jostling Daphne closer to Carter, then away.

A charge of awareness raced through her body. Fast, hard and very, very hot. The paper had proclaimed Carter the sexiest man in Indiana last year.

From where she sat, Daphne thought the reporter could have easily added a few states to that title. Maybe a whole continent.

Daphne drew in a breath, calming the charge of attraction. Playboys like him came with charisma included. She'd be smart to remember that.

They were nearly at the end of the trip. Daphne could easily keep her mouth shut now and let Carter go on his way. He had, after all, been at the root of the demise of her creativity center funding.

But something about the tense set of his shoulders, the lines in his forehead and the genuine worry in his eyes when he talked about his company tugged at her heartstrings.

He pulled up in front of the building that housed her office and parked the car. On the first floor, the bright green awning of Frankie's Delicatessen had already been unfurled for the day. The scent of Frankie's famous pot roast baking in preparation for the day's orders of roast beef sandwiches drifted through the car windows. "Here we are."

Daphne reached for the door handle. "Thanks."

"Wait," Carter said, reaching for her, his touch warm on her arm. He pivoted in his seat, his dark blue eyes studying hers. His tie, she noticed, was as neatly done as the rest of him. Not a Windsor out of place. "I'd like to hire you. As a way to make up for the whole basket thing, and—" he gave her the grin that the paper had once said should have been trademarked "—you can pull off the miracle I seem to have missed."

"You mean you want me to rescue your company while you sit by and watch?"

"Hell no," Carter chuckled. "I'll be on the golf course. Just send me the bill."

She let out a gust of frustration. "I don't think so." The door opened beneath her touch and a muttered, "Typical."

He'd blown it. He'd been Carter Matthews, the guy with the smile and the woman on his arm, not Carter Matthews, serious business owner in serious trouble. "Daphne, listen—"

She pivoted back. "Thanks for the ride. Why don't we just call it even? You can go back to your fun and games and I'll go back to my life."

"I wouldn't have asked you if I didn't need the help," he said, but he was sure by the look in her eyes that she was going to refuse him again.

"Uh-huh. Okay, then tell me. What's the current situation?" Daphne asked, hands on her hips. "How's production going? What's your profit margin? Your return customer ratio?"

"I'm not as familiar with production and…all that," he said. "I, ah, don't spend every day at the office."

She arched a brow. "How often *are* you in the office?"

Carter let out a little cough. "Twice a week." He paused. "In the mornings."

"Where are you when you aren't at work?"

"Networking," he said.

She looked at him, read his face as easily as a newspaper, then let out a snort. "You're golfing, aren't you?"

"Hey, I make very valuable business connections on the fairway."

"No wonder your company is failing, Mr. Matthews. To get a good pulse on your company, you really need to *be* there."

"I am…planning to," Carter added after a second. "Starting today."

"I can't help you." She threw up her hands. "I work with CEOs every day who are *committed* to turning their companies around. I don't want to work with someone who is just *playing* CEO."

"Is that how you see me?" he asked. "The stupid playboy who can't handle anything more complicated than taking down a woman's phone number?"

"Of course not. You can also handle a sports car. There's two great skills in life."

Her sarcasm ran through him like a knife. She, like most everyone else in his life, saw Carter as nothing more than his reputation.

Yet, he knew, just based on what he'd heard about Daphne, that she *could* help him turn around TweedleDee Toys. But as he took in Daphne Williams's heart-shaped face, he wondered if she might be a bit of a complication. Too pretty by half and far too distracting.

Regardless of how she looked or how she might distract him, TweedleDee Toys needed her expertise. Carter might not be toy-smart, but he was savvy enough to know when he needed to call in the cavalry.

"Despite what you think of me, will you help me?" he asked.

"No, Mr. Matthews, I won't. Not until you

stop looking at running a business as one big beach volleyball game." With that, the car door slammed shut and she was gone.

Carter sat back against the leather seat and sighed. What had Uncle Harry been thinking? Why would his uncle, who had set the playboy precedent in the Matthews family, name Carter as the heir of Tweedle-Dee Toys, one of Harry's many companies—or hobbies since he rarely did much more than dabble in something once he owned it—in his will?

Harry must have thought it would be the ultimate ha-ha on the Matthews family. Give the company to the one with the smallest sense of humor and see it tank. *That* was one to chuckle about at the next Thanksgiving dinner.

Despite his wealthy and crazy uncle's predictions, Carter wanted to see TweedleDee Toys succeed. Damn it all, he didn't just want it to succeed, he wanted it to corner twenty-five percent of the three-to-six-year-old market and thirty-percent of the preteens. They were lofty goals, but at the time he'd been full of fire and arrogance.

Nevertheless, he'd done his homework, putting those rusty college skills into practice. He'd arranged his goal sheets, set a chart of profit projections and sales quotas. The rest should have happened by now. But it hadn't.

Because as failure had become a bigger part of his day than success, he'd abandoned those lofty goals and starry-eyed ideas to play golf, unable to witness the company's demise.

Well, Carter wasn't going to sit by any longer. And maybe, if he could prove Daphne Williams wrong, then there was hope to turn the tide with all the other nay-sayers.

Reilly, Daphne's assistant, looked up from his desk when she walked in, his observant eyes studying her—and missing nothing. "You're looking awfully pensive this morning. And a tad ticked off."

"Who, me?" She affected a blank look.

"Yes, you." He crossed his arms over his bright purple shirt and maroon tie, a color combo that belied Reilly's fiftyish age. In a steady relationship with Elton, his "significant man" for more than twenty-five years, Reilly often acted more like a mother hen than an assistant. A nosy mother hen, Daphne amended, as Reilly's light green eyes narrowed to study her. "You also look… different. Did you meet someone? A new client? A nice guy?"

She refused to answer the question. Besides, she hadn't met a nice guy—just a guy with nice looks. "We have a meeting with the people from Lawford Community Bank in six minutes. I think we need to focus on that."

"No, we don't. They called five minutes ago and rescheduled for next Tuesday. Something about a surprise audit." Reilly crossed to a carafe sitting on the credenza behind his desk and poured them each a cup of coffee, handing one of the white mugs to Daphne. He perched on the edge of one of the desks. "So now we have some time and you can answer my question. Did you meet someone?"

"No." Daphne let out a laugh at the absurdity of the thought before taking a sip of the steaming brew. "Definitely no."

Reilly grinned. "I'd say definitely yes. The lady doth protest too much."

Daphne turned away and got busy hanging her purse on the coat tree by the door. "I wish you'd quit going to those Shakespeare in the Park productions. It gives you too many ideas. I swear, you're like a walking romance novel."

"Et tu Brute?" Reilly placed a hand over his heart and did his best to look stricken. "I thought you liked my poetic interpretations of the bard."

"Not when you're interpreting up the wrong tree." Daphne crossed the room, pulled her swivel chair up to her desk and began going through her stack of messages, the pile of pink While You Were Out papers fluttering like a skinny deck of cards. Satisfied there were no immediate emergencies, she laid the stack aside for later and then smoothed her hand over the oak top of the antique desk.

It had been her grandfather's and had survived everything from the Great Depression to Grandma Williams's Stickly phase.

But most of all, it was the only thing she

had left of the man who had inspired her, until he'd died when she was twelve. He'd been the one who had indulged her imagination, who hadn't scoffed at time spent staring off into space or drawing impossible inventions. He'd been the only one to encourage her to follow her dreams and find her niche, wherever it might lie.

Every morning when she sat down to work, she felt as if his spirit were welcoming her to the day. For that, Daphne treasured the desk.

"He wouldn't want you to be a work hermit, you know," Reilly said quietly, reading her mind. He pulled a chair up beside hers. "You're always here or off on some trip, helping a client."

"That's my job." She pressed the power button on her computer and waited for the PC to turn on.

"Yeah, but it's not your life. Your grandfather always wanted more for you." Reilly had never met her grandfather but had heard enough of Daphne's stories that he seemed to almost know him.

"I do, too, have a life. Or at least I used to before Jerry and I broke up."

Reilly laid a hand over hers. In the three years Reilly had worked for her, he and Elton had become her friends, complete with their Cher CD collection and miniature white poodle. It made for a warm workplace, and gave her a shoulder when things got too heavy for Daphne's own. There were many days when she was grateful she had hired the artistic and talented Reilly.

"I know. I'm sorry," he said, sincerity clear in his voice.

"How do you know? It just happened last night."

"Jerry was here first thing this morning. He stopped by to give you this." Reilly dropped a brochure for the creativity center onto her desk.

It had the symbol for Jerry's family foundation at the bottom. The words "Sponsored By" had been crossed out with a huge red X.

Well, that made it clear where he stood. Once again, Daphne was glad she was rid of a man like that. "I can't believe he did that. What a total jerk."

"Ditto," Reilly said. "What you need is a

nice guy. Preferably one with a whole lot of money he's looking to donate."

Carter Matthews had been nice, her mind whispered. *Gave you a ride to work, even though he was late.*

And he was cute. Very cute.

Daphne ignored her mental mutiny, double-clicked on Outlook and pretended to be interested in her schedule for the day. With the rescheduling of the Lawford Community Bank meeting, her day was depressingly empty. Too much time on her hands to think. To Daphne, being idle was never a good thing.

"What are you going to do about the funding for the creativity center?" Reilly asked. "Weren't you supposed to break ground on the thirtieth?"

"I'm going to call everyone I know. I'm sure at least one of the corporations we've worked with will put some money in."

"And do you have a backup plan?" Reilly asked, concern clear on his face. "Times have been tough in the last few years, so donations are harder to come by." He sighed. "I tell you, what you need is a rich man with nothing to do with his money but give it to you."

"I know one of those. Sort of."

A bad idea, considering how her mind brought up the image of Carter's eyes and that stubborn lock of hair again. She shook herself. All she needed was more than a granola bar for breakfast and Carter Matthews wouldn't get to her so easily.

"Really?" Reilly propped his chin into his hands, his ever-observant eyes watching her. "Who?"

"Carter Matthews." She turned away before Reilly—who she was sure was secretly psychic—could read anything in her eyes. "He gave me a ride to work today. After he totally screwed up my love life." She put up a hand at Reilly's question. "Don't ask. It's a long story."

"Ah-hah!" Reilly leaped to his feet and pointed at her. "That's what you were hiding this morning when you came in. You *like* him."

Reilly and Elton had made it their personal mission to see Daphne married—as soon as possible, so she could produce some small children for the childless couple to spoil. Reilly had never seen what he called "long-term breeding potential" in Jerry and had been on her case to find someone better.

She understood his concern, but had resisted his attempts to fix her up. A man only complicated matters. Jerry had been the perfect boyfriend—undemanding, and with few expectations.

Then why had that relationship left her feeling about as fulfilled as a Twinkie? Where the thought of Carter Matthews left her with the fullness of a seven-course meal?

"I met him, but don't go calling the preacher," she cautioned. "He's not someone I'd ever date—just a guy who owes me. Big time." She didn't tell Reilly the details. If she did, he'd feel inclined to put in his two cents—whether she wanted them or not.

When she'd hired Reilly Muldoon, she'd told him she wanted him to be an active voice in the company. She should have clarified how active that voice could be.

"Uh-huh. And this Carter—someone you aren't interested in at all, despite the fact that your face lit up just talking about him—you're really not interested in him?"

Her face had lit up? Jeez. She really needed more food in the morning.

"Not one bit."

Reilly wagged a finger at her. "I know interest, and honey, you have it all over your face. I say you should call him. Make the first move. Go after what you want."

"Reilly…" She gave up the admonishment and rolled her eyes. "You're impossible."

"And in my opinion—"

She put up a hand to stop him. "Which I didn't ask for."

As usual, Reilly went on, ignoring her. "If this guy had any brains at all and an ounce of testosterone, he'll be knocking on your door with wine, roses and a smile."

"He's a playboy, Reilly. A six-foot-tall, walking nightmare."

"So you noticed his height?" Reilly asked, grinning. "Anything else?"

"No, nothing. Now leave me alone."

"You never know." Reilly tick-tocked his finger at her. "This playboy might just be the one."

"The one for what?"

"The one to win your heart." He clutched his own chest and let out a dramatic sigh.

That would never happen. Daphne had made sure that particular piece of her anatomy wasn't up for grabs.

CHAPTER THREE

CARTER sat at his desk, holding the latest toy prototype for the Christmas catalog and let out a gust of frustration. At this point, he almost preferred the cat disaster.

Almost.

"*This* is what I pay you guys to come up with?" Carter turned the twelve-inch doll over. "An action figure that *cleans?*"

Paul Simmons, the former assistant head of the toy team, newly promoted to head designer after Jim's quick exit earlier today, sat back in the opposite chair and gestured toward the skinny, apron-clad male figurine. The doll carried a feather duster in one hand and a blue spray bottle in the other. "That's not just *any* action figure. It's SuperClean Man," he said, clearly proud of his team's creation. "He can sweep a floor in one fell swoop. Leap over three filled water buckets in a single bound and stop a speeding muddy dog with his bare hands."

Carter held himself back from rolling his eyes. A good CEO would show support for his staff. Get right behind them with window cleaner and a good rag. "I thought we decided to come up with a toy that would make little boys aspire to big things. A role model of sorts."

"SuperClean Man's a role model," Paul said. "He can bring home the bacon—"

"And fry it up in the pan," Carter finished. He reached forward to straighten a pen on his desk, setting it to rights beside the pad of paper. Order made him feel better.

A little.

Neatness at least gave the impression he knew what he was doing. That he had some use in this office besides taking up Uncle Harry's leather chair. Uncle Harry's office had been a disaster when Carter took over, stuffed to the brim with gag gifts, like a toilet that served as a bank, complete with a flushing sound whenever you deposited a quarter. A pair of teeth that chattered across the desk. A clown head that laughed if you clapped twice. Carter had left most of the jokester material in his office, hoping the funnies might inspire good ideas.

They hadn't. Especially if this mopping doll was any indication.

"SuperClean Man can also scrub the hell out of the grease stains behind the stove." Paul grinned.

Now Carter did roll his eyes heavenward, praying for patience. He didn't receive any patience or inspiration. At this point, he'd settle for a bolt of lightning to put him out of his misery.

"So, is he a go?" Paul asked. "I think the preschool boys will really love him."

"For what? Mopping up after Spider-Man saves the day?"

Paul shifted in his chair. "He can vacuum, too. That's cool, isn't it?"

Carter sighed.

"I hear Barbie's looking for a new guy since she dumped Ken," Paul said, a hopeful gleam in his eye.

Carter tossed SuperClean Man at Paul,

then restacked a pile of papers on his desk. "Get this thing out of my sight."

Paul stood, toying with the man-maid. "Does this mean we aren't getting Super-Clean Man on the assembly line?"

"No, but he might join *you* on the janitorial staff if you don't give me a better idea." Carter popped forward in his chair, his gaze hardening. "Today."

Paul nodded and backed out of the door faster than a cat being chased by a bulldog.

Carter drummed his fingers on his desk and glanced at the phone. He needed help. No, he needed a miracle. He was in way over his head, had been since he'd inherited the company from Uncle Harry two months ago. Although he and Uncle Harry had shared a lot of laughs whenever they were together, the two peas from the same pod, he couldn't imagine why his uncle saw Carter as CEO material. Uncle Harry had always said Carter could be more than he was, but given the fact that Uncle Harry usually sported a red nose that beeped when he made declarations like that, Carter had never taken him seriously.

And now, he was in a serious mess. Carter

didn't know anything about toys. Heck, he barely knew how to play with one. But Daphne Williams—

He suspected *she* knew how to have fun. Something about the twinkle in her eye, the laughter that lingered beneath her voice— when she wasn't angry with him—told him she held the key to what he needed.

He cut off any thoughts of dating Daphne. Cecilia's breakup basket was a clear sign he wasn't good at relationships. Longevity wasn't his long suit, not given his background. If relationship dysfunction could be a family trait, Carter was sure he'd inherited it, along with his father's cowlick.

Cade had been lucky—he'd avoided the cowlick and ended up with far better relationship abilities. He and Melanie had been married for nearly twenty years now, a feat by anyone's standards.

The last thing Carter wanted to do right now was get involved. Hell, his own life was messy enough. He didn't need to complicate anyone else's.

But he *did* need Daphne Williams. If

anything, today's adventures with the mopping man-doll had proven that to him.

Considering his only other choice was manufacturing a line of plastic Stepford Husbands, he figured helping Daphne find some funding wasn't a bad choice.

He reached for the phone, but didn't pick up the receiver. No. He wouldn't call. He'd go in person. He liked the way she glared at him and the way she tried so hard to stay out of his personal space when they'd been in his car. Everything about her body language said stay away, yet—

She needed him and he needed her.

What we have here is a quandary. Now, throw the two of us together again and see where a little mixing of personalities ends up.

Hopefully with something better than SuperClean Man and his little plastic mop bucket.

"That's not a lunch," Reilly said. "It's a snack."

Daphne kept on typing, ignoring Reilly's well-meaning advice, and the paltry meal sitting beside her. "I don't have time for lunch. Plus, I have a beverage and something from two of the four food groups."

"A diet soda and a package of cheese crackers does not qualify as a meal." He gave her a frown. "You need real food. If you don't take care of you—"

She paused to laugh. "I can't take care of you."

Reilly grinned. "Exactly. And I need this job, so I can't have the boss keeling over from hunger."

Daphne looked at her lunch and wondered for a brief second what Carter Matthews was eating right now. Probably a tuna salad neatly arranged on a rye, with nary a lettuce leaf out of place, served by some buxom blonde who would laugh at all his jokes and consider his smile tip enough.

Or perhaps, something good and greasy, and bad for his arteries. A cheeseburger. A plate of spaghetti with extra meatballs, all the better to stuff his ego.

Maybe he'd drip a little grease on his tie. Or some crumbs onto his starched white shirt. It would serve him right for questioning her like that.

Yet, her mind refused to see him with bread fragments on his button-down shirt. Instead images of him taking a bite, then sharing another bite with her like they were Romans reclining and dining on grapes, seemed to crop up with annoying frequency.

Reilly was right. She needed to eat more.

But not with Carter. If there was anything a man like Carter Matthews spelled, especially after that message from Cecilia, it was a broken heart.

Her stomach rumbled, reminding her that despite her best laid plans, her love life—and her belly—were both dismally empty at the same time.

"Did someone say lunch?"

Daphne jerked her head up, half expecting to see Kim in the doorway and finding instead—

Carter Matthews.

Clearly God had a sense of humor.

The sight of him socked her in the gut. Twice in one day. It had to be some kind of cosmic mix-up or a heck of a twist to the laws of life by Murphy himself.

Carter looked as delicious as cookies and

milk. As inviting as a smorgasbord of chocolate. Hunger of another kind growled in Daphne's gut.

She ran a hand over her hair, smoothing it into place, then adjusted her glasses. "What are you doing here?"

He grinned. "Taking my creativity coach out to lunch."

"I'm not your creativity coach. And as for lunch, I can't. I have to—"

"She can, she can," Reilly said, turning Daphne's chair and rolling it in Carter's direction. "Don't let her tell you no."

She put her foot down, putting some brakes on Reilly before he rolled her right into Carter's arms. "Reilly!"

"You need to eat and he's offering a meal," Reilly said into her ear. "Seems like a match made in heaven."

"You're fired," she muttered.

"That's twice this week," he said with a grin. "You're getting soft in your old age. Last week you fired me three times."

She gave him a glare, then got up, since Reilly wasn't going to let her go back to her crackers and soda, not without a fight. She was outnumbered. When her stomach rumbled a second time, she knew she didn't stand a chance in this battle. "Okay, a quick lunch, a hot dog from the vendor on Seventh. That's it."

Carter shook his head. "Sorry. You made a deal. You want my undivided attention, I want yours."

Her attention had been—and still was—divided. Daphne needed to concentrate on her business and the building of the creativity center, not Carter Matthews. Going to lunch with him—especially with him, a man whose teasing smile set off shock waves in her gut—would undoubtedly feel more like a date than a business transaction.

"I have work to do…" She gestured vaguely at the pile of work on her desk, the PC fired up with at least a half-dozen open programs. Even though it looked like a busy day, she knew her schedule was pretty clear, since that meeting had been canceled. Still, given half a second, she could find plenty of ways to fill the time.

Anything to avoid Carter Matthews's piercing blue gaze that seemed to question everything about her. Carter took a step forward, his gaze connecting with hers, as if he'd read her mind. "Listen, I want to apologize for the way I acted in the car earlier. If you're available, I could really use a brilliant mind to pick. A free meal, and I promise to be on my best behavior. What do you say?"

"All right," she said, relenting to the growing gnawing feeling in her stomach.

He grinned. "Now those are my two favorite words in the world. The more you say them, the happier I'll be."

"I have another two words in mind for you," she muttered.

"Careful," Carter said, wagging a mocking finger at her, "your attitude is showing."

"That's only because you bring out the worst in me."

From the sidelines, Reilly watched the entire exchange with clear amusement. He didn't even pretend to be busy, just sat at his desk, sipping a glass of water and eavesdropping with glee.

She'd have to remember to cut back his benefits.

Daphne figured she'd better leave now or

risk having her entire plan exposed to Reilly's eagle eyes—and his penchant for commentary. "Let's go to lunch, Mr. Matthews."

"First, let's call a truce." He put out his hand. She took it and felt the warmth of his palm engulf her own. Once again, the charge of attraction erupted inside her.

"By the way, you have a great office here," Carter said, looking around the wide loft space. "I should hire you to decorate mine."

"Thank you."

"Did you do it yourself?"

She chuckled. "When you're a new business owner, everything is done yourself. When I first opened, it was just me, so I spent a lot of late nights inside this space, painting and decorating. It used to be a warehouse and had been abandoned for a couple years before I rented out this floor, so it needed a lot of TLC." She grinned. "I also spent a lot of time cursing old buildings and their surprises behind every wall."

"I think it's cool. Really cool. And evocative of you, your personality."

She pivoted, seeing her fifth-floor offices through Carter's eyes—the paint that played from orange to yellow to red as he pivoted around the room, the rainbow-colored pillars that hid the pipes and structural beams. Across the room, a basketball hoop hung on one wall, a Velcro dartboard on another. A multicolored sofa with pillows of all shapes and sizes promised comfort against the far wall, flanked by a pair of whimsical wooden end tables, one of a waiter cutout holding a tray and a dog holding a newspaper on the opposite side.

"If I had a space like this," Carter said, "I might get a little more out of my people. Uncle Harry's office is a little…drab."

"Uncle Harry?" she said, turning the knob and opening the door, leading the way out to the hall. Behind her, she caught a quick thumbs-up from Reilly, which she chose to ignore.

"I inherited the company from him. He never sat in the office, or at least not very often, so I doubt he noticed how dark it was. Uncle Harry liked his 'investments' as he called them, just not spending much time with them. He was more interested in pursuing a part-time career in stand-up."

"Seriously?"

Carter nodded. "Uncle Harry loved a good joke more than anything else. But he did give me my sense of humor and was a heck of an entertaining baby-sitter, whenever he was in town."

"I guess that partly explains the shape the company is in now."

Carter pushed the down button on the elevator bank, then stood back to wait, as stiff in his demeanor as a military officer. "That and he didn't exactly pick the right man to run it."

She glanced at him, surprised. "I'm sure he wouldn't have put you in charge if he didn't think you were the right man for the job."

"Let's just say Uncle Harry never passed up the opportunity for a good practical joke, even from the grave."

The elevator doors opened and they stepped into the ornate, old machine. It shivered a little on its trip down the five floors, rattling the mirror on the wall. "Old buildings," Daphne explained.

"Lots of character."

"And a nice high maintenance bill." She grinned. "My creativity in design is really creativity for my pocketbook. Dark paint covers up water stains pretty well."

He laughed. "I do like the way you think, Daphne Williams."

They exited the elevator, entering the bright, carpeted lobby and pushed through the double glass doors onto the street. The smells of Frankie's Delicatessen, stronger now with the lunch menu in full swing, wafted over to greet them.

"The deli's great," Daphne said, "but I think for what we need to accomplish today, we'll need to talk somewhere quieter."

My apartment, Carter's mind suggested. He gave his hormones a mental slug. He was supposed to be thinking about Daphne in business terms only. Nothing more.

But when he turned and took in her tall, slim shape, the long, easy strides of her graceful legs and the quiet clicks of her strappy heels, he couldn't think of much beyond his apartment and getting her there.

He reminded himself that he had allotted

a little over an hour for this meeting, enough time to lay out his biggest problems then get back to the office for another, hopefully not as fruitless, meeting with the toy designers. He didn't have time for anything more than a conversation with Daphne, even if he did give in to his baser desires.

Still, his gaze traveled up, over the trim cobalt suit she wore, past the slash of the lime tank beneath the jacket, to capture her heart-shaped face, framed as prettily as a photo by the smooth length of her dark brown hair.

"Mr. Matthews? I asked you a question. Twice."

"Oh, sorry. I was…daydreaming."

"I asked you if you liked Italian."

With you, yes. Alone? Not so much.

He recovered his manners and his business face, clearly lost somewhere between his journey up the elevator to her office and the journey back down. Carter straightened his tie and smoothed his suit jacket. The movements helped him feel a little more in control, the place where Carter Matthews was most at ease. And where he had learned he kept bad memories at bay. "Italian would be great. Were you thinking of—"

"Lombardo's?" they both said at the same time.

He chuckled. "Great minds think alike."

"Or it could be that it's the only decent Italian restaurant in downtown Lawford," she said, clearly not giving him an inch.

He didn't want an inch, he reminded himself. Business only. Relationships—and toys that didn't die or clean with a vengeance—were his weak point.

And so was Daphne Williams, without a doubt.

CHAPTER FOUR

THE mundane activities of ordering pasta and side salads gave Daphne a little bit of distance from her hormones, which were staging a huge protest about her decision to think of Carter Matthews as nothing more than a potential client, a lunch companion. But as she glanced over at him, she knew she was lying to herself.

"You fascinate me," Carter said, after the waitress took away their salad plates.

"Really?" A little laugh escaped her, as she worked on quieting those hormones, now all in a tizzy again. "How's that?"

"You're a successful business owner, and you seem so…together with the whole thing. Half the time I feel lost, and the other half, I don't know what to do."

She grinned. "It gets easier. My first year

was hard, with lots of mistakes, but they were great learning experiences."

He snorted. "I'm learning this might not be my forte."

"Maybe. Maybe not. You'll never know unless you stick it out."

"True." He cocked his head and studied her, the perusal once again setting off a surge of want inside her. "Do you always have all the right answers, Miss Williams?"

She laughed. "In business, sometimes. In life, not so much."

"Isn't it that way for everyone, though? We all drive down the road, but we're never sure if we took the right turns along the way."

"Until we get to the end and see we totally screwed it up."

He laughed, and they shared a smile of connection. She realized she liked Carter Matthews—not in the dating sense, but as a person. He had a good sense of humor and a keen observation of people—even if she was the one under the Carter microscope.

He took a sip of his iced tea, then caught her gaze. "Daphne, I'm serious about hiring you to help me with my company. I need a miracle."

"I don't have time right now." Not a total lie, more an excuse to put a lot more distance between her and Carter Matthews. "I'm in major fund-raising mode right now."

He arched a brow. "Fund-raising? For what?"

"A creativity center for children."

"You need an entire center to inspire creativity in kids? Can't you just give them some paper and a couple Crayolas?"

What had she expected? That she'd tell a man like Carter about her life's mission and he'd take her seriously? *"Crayolas? Paper? Forget I even mentioned it."* She started to rise. "This was a mistake."

He reached across the table for her hand, urging her back into her seat. "I'm sorry."

Two words and Daphne was sinking back into the cushy vinyl seat. What was it about this man that made her keep thinking there was something else beneath the playboy surface?

"I jumped to conclusions and for that, I apologize." Carter crossed his hands over each other and met her gaze. "Tell me more about this center."

"You really want to know?"

"Yes, I really do. Maybe I'll send my toy designers there. They need something that will take them out of their current paper doll and stick figure thinking."

She laughed. "Well, when I was a kid, I had a grandfather who really encouraged me. He let me be creative, really think outside the box, whenever I visited him."

"Sounds like a great guy."

"He was." She sighed. Grandfather Wallace hadn't been around nearly as often as she would have liked. Nor had he lived long enough to rescue her from a life of chaos or from Daphne's mother walking out, then walking back into her life, as if motherhood were a revolving door.

"Anyway," Daphne went on, brushing aside the thoughts, "I've always dreamed of creating a place where kids could develop their imaginations, their artistic talents. To bring something vibrant and stimulating to the downtown area, to these kids' lives. Too often, art is the first thing cut from school programs. Creativity gets stifled at the expense of the three R's."

"Well, those three R's are pretty important."

"They are," Daphne agreed, thanking the waitress as she deposited their dishes of pasta on the table. "But if you don't have creativity, how will you ever go beyond the basics? Without encouraging creative thinking, we'll lose out on the next Da Vinci or Rembrandt or Einstein."

"Or Daphne Williams." He grinned.

Heat flooded her cheeks and she dug into her food. "I'm not like them. I'm just—"

"Don't," Carter said. "Don't push the compliment away. They're a rarity where I come from."

He said the words with a joke in his voice, but Daphne had to wonder. The golden playboy's life seemed a little tarnished. Perhaps there was more to Carter Matthews than met the eye—and the newspaper headlines. "Then thank you."

His smile widened. "Perfect."

"With this center, I want to create a place where kids can feel at home, feel the freedom of an idea-generating environment. One that welcomes differences, rather than crushing them." That, Daphne knew, was the only way to give the next generation the tools it needed to expand their thinking, come up with innovative ideas. She'd had her grandfather—but not every little girl did. "But for that to happen, I have to find funding. Fast. Groundbreaking is in two weeks."

"Didn't you have a foundation or corporate support already lined up?"

"I did. Then someone's Breakup Basket made me sever that relationship."

"Oh." Guilt rocketed through Carter. He'd seen the excitement in Daphne's eyes as she talked about her center, and to think he'd been part of ruining it… He couldn't have been a bigger heel if he'd been the end of a loaf of French bread. "I'm sorry. Really sorry."

She shrugged, as if it didn't matter, but he could see that it did. "I'm planning on calling all my old clients. See if I can find some corporate sponsors. With Jerry backing out, I don't have enough financing to do more than turn over a spade of dirt."

They grew silent a moment, each taking the time to eat. If Carter had had a place like what Daphne was talking about when he was a kid, would it have made a difference? Would it have provided the environment that had been lacking from his home?

And would it have prepared him for the mess he found himself in now? A mess that was quickly spiraling into the failure his father had predicted.

Carter refused to let those predictions come true. He would make this company a success, even if it killed him. "What if you only came in and worked with my guys for one day? Would that work in your schedule?"

"I really can't," she said, pushing her plate to the side. "I have clients to attend to, the fund-raising effort."

"Or is the real reason that you don't want to work with me?"

"That's ridiculous." Daphne fished in her purse, came up with her half of the bill and laid the money on the table. "Now, if you'll excuse me, Mr. Matthews, I really have to get back to work."

She rose and then turned to leave. Damn. He had yet to convince her how desperately he needed her. He threw a few more bills on the table, then caught up with her inside the crowded lobby. "What if I help you with the creativity center?"

She turned around. "Help me? How?"

"After it's built, I'll fill it with the best toys. Bring my designers in to talk to the kids about a career in toys." He could see the idea wheels turning in her head. More people slipped into the restaurant, filling the small lobby space, forcing Daphne and Carter to the side, into the space between the hostess desk and the wall. It was a dark little alcove, one of those designing mistakes that made for empty space. And very close quarters. "I promise, I won't take much of your time. Just enough to get me past this rough spot."

"I appreciate the great offer, but I'm not so sure working together is such a good idea." Daphne's chin turned up to meet his, so close, he could have kissed her with no effort at all.

"Why?" But in the beat of his heart, the fire simmering in his belly, he knew why.

"Because…" She swallowed. "It could get complicated."

A pair of businessmen crowded in on the other side, oblivious to their briefcases pushing into the space occupied by Daphne and Carter. She shifted closer to him, avoiding a collision.

"Oh, yeah. Very complicated," Carter said. He could feel her every breath against his chest, inhale the sweet, cinnamony scent of her perfume, feel the soft texture of her skirt when she moved.

"Carter, we should…" But she didn't finish the sentence. Didn't move. Didn't leave their small microcosm.

He glanced down, capturing her chestnut gaze. Outside of their little space, the world moved on, diner's names were called, orders were placed, meals were eaten. But here, in the tight, dark corner, Carter saw and heard nothing but Daphne. He forgot his reason for being there.

Forgot everything but her.

The businessmen shuffled a step back to make room for someone else, forcing Daphne against Carter's chest. That contact was all it took to take him from interested to needing her. He swallowed, knowing how wrong it would be to mix business and pleasure.

But wanting nothing more than the pleasure of her mouth beneath his.

He'd kissed dozens of women in his lifetime. Had just as many who had kissed him first. But never had he felt such an intense stirring of desire, as if Daphne was the one Christmas present he'd never received.

"We should probably leave," he said, trying to do the right thing. For once.

"Yeah," she answered, but her mouth didn't shut at the end of the word, and Carter's best intentions disappeared.

One of them, or both of them, it seemed, closed the final distance. She kissed him— and he kissed her, and something within Carter, some long sleeping need, exploded. It slammed into him in multiplied waves he couldn't remember feeling for a woman in a long, long time.

Her lips still held the sweet taste of the cherry soda she'd drank with her lunch, the

softness of a woman, the temptation of for-
bidden fruit.

His arms stole around her back, one hand
reaching up to cup the back of her head,
tangling in the length of her soft brown hair,
the other pressing against that valley above
her waist, the sweet dip where her back
curved toward him and he knew, that with the
slightest bit of pressure, she'd be close
enough to really push him over the edge
from need to agony.

Before their kiss could go anywhere near
agony territory, he came to his senses and
pulled back. "Sorry, I don't know what
happened there."

"Yeah, me neither," she said, her lips red
and plump and so clearly freshly kissed that
he wanted to do it again.

Carter had thought perhaps that by kissing
her, it would answer the questions his
hormones were asking. If anything, kissing
Daphne had stirred up even more.

"This is why we can't work together." She
worried her bottom lip and all he could think
about was kissing her a second time.

"Those complications, right?"

"And you, Mr. Matthews, come with far too many of them." Daphne bade him goodbye and worked her way through the crowd and out the exit. Leaving Carter wishing he'd had the creativity to think of a way to get her to stay.

Carter got back to his office and knew this arrangement with Daphne Williams was never going to work.

For one, he'd kissed her.

For another, he'd enjoyed the kiss.

And for a third, he'd totally blown any discussion of his company's needs because all his thoughts had been on—

Kissing her again.

Getting to know her. Seeing her smile. Seeing the excitement that flared in her eyes, her cheeks, when she talked about the things most important to her.

Daphne was a distraction, something Carter had far too much experience with. What he needed now was focus, not a woman who would set his hormones afire.

"Mr. Matthews, you don't need me." Pearl Jenkins, his assistant, sat at the opposite end of his desk, poring over the first quarter financials.

"Pearl, I need you more than I need my right arm. The only experience I have with profit and loss is running my Visa through the little black machine at the department stores."

Pearl didn't spare him a laugh. The woman was as severe and straight as her gray hair, as neat as a pin in her work, and as serious as a heart attack about her job. "What you need, if you don't mind me saying so, is a miracle." She ran her gaze down the sheet of numbers again. "A visit from a saint and a few favors from the whole host of heavenly angels might be a good idea, too."

"It's that bad?"

She arched a darkly penciled brow. "You know what happened to the Titanic?"

He nodded.

"That would be a *happy* ending compared to what's happening to TweedleDee Toys." Pearl picked up the narrow bifocals she wore on a beaded chain around her neck, slipped them onto her nose, then began reciting numbers, each one on the negative end of the spectrum.

Dread sunk to the pit of his stomach. He'd known things were bad. He just hadn't thought they were this bad. When Pearl finally stopped verbally spreading the entrails of TweedleDee across her spreadsheet, Carter drew in a breath. "We need to stem the gushing as much as possible," he said. "First, no overtime. Second, I want to see a breakdown of labor by department, as well as its profitability—"

She handed him several slips of paper. At TweedleDee, Pearl was the only efficient cog in the machine.

"Thanks. I suppose you already have projections for next quarter?"

She nodded, and gave him another sheet. "I hope you like the color red," she said, with a brief snippet of a smile.

"Let's—" The buzzer on his intercom cut him off. "Yes?"

"Mr. Matthews?" Sally called. The receptionist's nasal voice seemed to fill the phone, compounded by her cold. "Your father is here to see you."

"Will do."

"I'm taking a couple days off. I think I have—" she coughed into the intercom "—a sinus infection. I'll get you a temp."

Carter thanked her, then wished her a fast recovery. He sat back and prepared for the visit of his father. If there was anything that could possibly worsen his day, the arrival of Jonathon Matthews was it. "Send him in."

Pearl gathered her papers, gave Carter a sympathetic smile, then left the room, letting Jonathon in as she did. Carter straightened in his seat, his hand automatically going to his tie, before he chided himself for worrying about what his father would think of his appearance.

He was, after all, only a few years from forty. What his father thought of him shouldn't matter.

But damn it, it did.

"Carter," Jonathon said, his voice sharp and direct. He cut a tall and imposing figure in a dark blue pin-striped suit and shoes that shone like mirrors. "What the hell do you think you're doing?"

"Trying to run a company." Carter waved a hand at the space around him. "I have the office, the suit and even my nameplate on my desk. That makes me the guy in charge."

His father snorted, then lowered himself into one of the chairs opposite Carter. Even seated, Jonathon gave off the air of a lion. "What you're doing is running it into the ground, from what I hear."

Carter didn't reply.

"Listen, I know you. This business is just another shiny toy." Jonathon laughed at his pun. "Soon as the next shiny one comes along—most likely one with a nice pair of legs and no need for commitment—you'll bail. Why don't you just give up this foolish business now? Let your brother run it or better yet, hire a competent CEO."

Meaning Carter was the opposite of competent, at least in his father's eyes. When he'd been a kid, if there'd been a broken vase, Carter had been the first Jonathon blamed. When report cards came out, Jonathon had gushed over Cade's, then reluctantly asked for Carter's, knowing it wouldn't measure up to his twin's. No matter what Carter had done, it had been less than good enough. Uncle Harry had been the only one who'd been in Carter's corner—albeit with a whoopee cushion and a water-squirting flower.

"For one," Carter said, "Cade is busy with Melanie and helping her build the franchise of her coffee shop. For another, I am fully capable of handling this company."

"The only thing you've ever handled is women, and even then I've had to bail you out."

Carter bristled. "I'll never be good enough, will I?"

His father picked an invisible bit of lint off his trousers, then faced his son. "When you do as your brother has, then maybe you'll make up for thirty-seven years of screw-ups."

Carter's only betrayal of his temper was a tightening of his jaw and the clenched fist that rested on the arm of his chair. "So that's it? I get married and you'll see me as something other than the family disgrace?"

"It would be a start, yes. And, it wouldn't hurt you with this business."

"How does my marital status make a difference with TweedleDee Toys?"

"Face it, Carter, your reputation got here before you. The scuttlebutt around town is that you're about as reliable as a wet piece of tape. If you settled down, maybe customers might be more willing to invest their dollars in a company they believe has some longevity. Right now, they're running away as fast as they can because they want to make sure—" at this, his father's light blue eyes met his, direct and unflinching "—that this CEO thing isn't 'another passing fancy.'"

Carter winced at the words, a direct quote from the Indianapolis newspapers which had reported on his recent ownership of the company. His father was right—and if there was one thing that annoyed Carter, it was his father being right. Years of being the playboy, the careless heir to a small family legacy, had made him the darling of the papers. To the point where they took him about as seriously as an ice-cream cone. Every date, every misstep, was splashed across the pages. On a slow news day, he even merited TV coverage. "Carter Matthews is at it again," the reporter would start, then detail his latest escapade.

He'd become the Paris Hilton of the Midwest. Except his family fortune was a mere drop in the bucket and no one had asked him to do a sexy car washing commercial.

His father rose. "The smartest thing you can do is get married and hire someone who knows what they're doing to run this place. And do it fast because your customers are deserting you faster than they ran away at Pompeii."

On that note, his father left. Carter's gaze dropped to the profit and loss statement on his desk. The red screamed back at him, like a patient hemorrhaging on an operating table.

In two weeks, maybe three, there wouldn't be enough money to make payroll. He thought of Paul. He'd met the toy designer's wife and two kids last week. Mike had a mother in the hospital. Pearl was the sole breadwinner, providing for her and her husband and a daughter who had returned home after an ugly divorce.

These people were counting on him to pay their checks. Keep them employed. And most of all, keep TweedleDee Toys running.

Nothing like a little pressure.

Daphne Williams's business card sat to the right of his phone, the bright, primary colors speaking as loudly as the woman's personality. She needed help; he needed respectability—

And rescue.

An idea flitted through Carter's mind, one that was surely as crazy as the SuperClean Man.

But if it worked—

It'd sure clean up the mess that surrounded him right now.

Daphne hung up the phone and let out a gust of frustration. "Another no," she told Reilly.

"Honey, someone will say yes."

"Yeah, in about ten years. I want to get this funding now so I can make a difference for *this* generation. Not for my grandkids."

Reilly gave her a grin. "You'd have to actually spend more than five minutes with a man in order to have grandkids."

She rolled her eyes and ignored him. "All these companies are more than happy to hire me for creativity seminars, but when it comes to parting with donation dollars, you'd think

I was asking the CEO to cut off his right arm."

"Was that the last one of our former clients?" Reilly asked, gesturing to the phone.

"Yep. After this, it's cold calling. And we all know how well that goes over. What I need is a—"

"A rich angel," Reilly finished.

She grinned. "Do you know any of those?"

"Actually…" Reilly began, affecting an innocent face, "I know a single man who likes you and who has huge media potential. Meaning he could attract the kind of PR you need to get other companies on board."

Carter Matthews.

As mistakes went, Carter was a T-Rex-size mistake, poised to grow to Texas-size. She wanted to go back to the restaurant, take back that kiss. Get a do-over.

"You know, having a toy company would be a great boost for business," Reilly said. "What better way to sell yourself as a creativity coach than by getting TweedleDee Toys back into the game?"

"I don't have time for him. Or his company."

Well, she had had time earlier today—plenty

of it—when he'd drawn her into his arms for that impetuous kiss. Also a giant mistake.

She may be loose and creative in her workshops, but when it came to her personal life, Daphne stayed as far away from spontaneity as possible.

Until Carter had come along and awakened a long dormant need inside her. Kissing him had only added complications, like too much cayenne in an already volatile chili.

She wasn't about to tell Reilly that, though. The minute she did, Reilly would be arranging for the preacher and the church.

"Speaking of the devil. Look who's here again," Reilly said, gesturing toward the video screen that captured the lobby of the building. "Mr. Available."

Daphne shot Reilly a look of annoyance, then found her hand straying to smooth her hair. She caught Reilly grinning and yanked her hand away. "Stop playing matchmaker or I'll dock your pay."

"Promises, promises," Reilly said, grinning. He turned toward his computer and went back to work. Daphne could swear she could hear him humming a love song under his breath.

She rose when Carter entered the office, striding across the room, cool and professional, as if that kiss had never happened. Yet, it still echoed within her. Her mind had returned to it again and again this afternoon, disturbing her line of thought a hundred times over. "Mr. Matthews. Back so soon?"

"I have an…offer of sorts to make you, one that will hopefully change your mind about working with my company."

"Are you determined or a glutton for punishment? I already said no."

"Both," Carter said. "But I'd like to try one more time to, ah, persuade you. It seems I didn't make a strong enough case at lunch."

Heat inflamed Daphne's cheeks. Oh, he'd made a strong case, all right. One for turning him down once and for all, before she did something stupid, like date him.

Reilly turned around, one brow raised in question, an I-told-you-so grin eating up his face. "Let's go into the conference room," she said, "and we can do that in private."

Reilly let out a cough.

"I meant, discuss your *company* in private," Daphne corrected, but the damage had already been done. A slight smile lingered on Carter's lips, while Reilly had increased his humming volume.

She pivoted and led the way to the conference room at the back of the office space, grabbing a pad of paper off her desk as she headed into the conference room. The door shut behind Carter.

They were alone.

Entirely alone.

Her mind, never at a lack for creative ideas, supplied several involving her and Carter and the very long and very available conference table. Daphne pushed—no, shoved—those thoughts aside and sat down on one side of the table, waited while Carter took the other, then got right down to business.

Instead of looking at him and remembering how good that man could kiss.

"Listen, Mr. Matthews—"

"Carter, please."

"Carter," she said, the name slipping off her tongue far too easily. "Why don't I just give you a few quick tips that you can employ with your staff. Then you can find another creativity coach at your leisure."

"I like the one I already have."

She ignored him. "Tell me your specific problems, so I can give you the best exercises to conquer them. We didn't really get a chance to talk at lunch."

That was because the entire meal had been spent with her trying to avoid his gaze and keeping her hormones in check. If he'd said anything at all to her, it had flitted away, evaporating in the heat between them.

He laid his hands flat on the table before him. "At this point, I'm desperate. My toy designers haven't come up with a decent idea in six months, and sales of our existing products are flattening out, in some cases dropping, because there's nothing new to catch the public's fancy. We're a few checks away from shutting our doors. The fall toy rollout is in a few weeks, and if we can have something amazing by then, we'll have enough preorders to save the company." He steepled his fingers, then pressed them to his chin. "But I don't know diddly about toys, so I'm no help."

She grinned. "Well, surely you had some G.I. Joes or puzzles or something as a kid."

He shook his head. "Not me."

He didn't elaborate and she didn't push it. Instead she asked him some basic specific information—how long the company had been in existence, how many toy designers he had and what niche the company focused on.

That question gave him the most pause. "We were heavily in the three-to-six-year-old market, but a year or so ago, my uncle up and decided there was more money in preteens. Thus far, we haven't had anything that's become a stand-out hit in either area."

"And are you looking to break into the preteen area or to continue growing with your core audience?"

Carter grinned. "Both. I guess I'd like TweedleDee to be successful in more than one market. Eggs in multiple baskets, as they say."

Daphne made a note, then sat back in her chair. "I'd suggest three things—you should hold a meeting with your toy designers to really get a feel for them and their personalities, if you haven't already. Then I can give you a sheet of in-office creativity exercises—"

He waved off the suggestion. "I heard you do retreats."

"Well, yes. I often take clients and their staffs to my house in Maine for a two-day intensive retreat. It's for the more drastic cases."

"That's what I want then."

"I already told you I can't."

He grabbed the pad in front of her, then took a pen from his breast pocket and circled the words "forty-five percent loss." "Wouldn't you say these are drastic times?"

Even she could see that. "Yes."

"Good, we finally agree on something." He sat back and flashed that smile at her again. Her resistance began to erode. "I talked to John Matthews, who owns that marketing agency on Fifth. He couldn't sing your praises loud enough. You are clearly passionate about what you do. I saw you light up when you talked about that creativity center. That's the kind of excitement I want to breed within my own company, with your help. To do that, I want to offer you a deal, a much bigger deal than just donating a bunch of toys to your center."

"A deal?" Daphne paused, her pen tight in her grip. "What kind of deal?"

"I help you find your funding and you help my company."

She cocked her head. "And how are you going to help me find my funding?"

"Trust me. No one has more connections with the wealthy in this area than the baddest playboy in Indiana." He said the words as a joke, but they seemed to hit awfully close to a sensitive bone. Carter brushed the feeling off.

Skepticism shone in her eyes. "And you'd be willing to use these connections to help me?"

"As long as you help me."

Of course, Carter wasn't so sure he knew *how* to find funding for a creativity center, considering he'd spent more of his life spending money than making it, and his idea of supporting a charity was securing a date for the annual Children's Fund Ball. But he wasn't going to tell Daphne that. Surely a few well-placed phone calls and a couple of golf games could bring about the networking she needed.

Across from him, Daphne hesitated. Were the same doubts running through her mind?

"I don't know. What's the catch?"

Carter leaned forward. "You still have to help me, even if this Jerry comes back and brings in the funding, along with a ring and some wedding bells."

At that, her face paled. "Oh, no, believe me, that won't happen. Especially the wedding bells part."

"You weren't planning on marrying him?" The interest, and its accompanying idea, that had been brewing in his veins perked up a bit more.

"Well…it's a little soon and we weren't dating all that long and…" She drew herself up. "And it's none of your business."

He smiled. "No, it isn't. But if we're going to do this, then we'll be in each other's business a whole lot very soon."

Her moist pink lips opened, then shut. Carter wondered for a second whether he'd just proposed this idea to help his company—

Or for something else a heck of a lot more personal.

She studied him. "What does my love life— or lack thereof—have to do with all this?"

The air between them went quiet, the room falling silent save for the sound of Reilly typing beyond the door. "Because I want to marry you."

He put the words so plainly, he could have said, "I want roast beef on rye." Daphne blinked, hesitating while she replayed the words again. "You *what?*"

"Want to marry you." He put up a hand to head off her objections. "It's more of a business deal than anything else."

She laughed. "Gee, what a romantic. Sorry, Mr. Matthews. I won't marry you just so you can get out of paying my fee."

"That wasn't my intention, believe me." He chuckled. "You and I both need something, and I propose this as a solution."

"And what is it that I need from you?" she said. Her mind volunteered a mini movie of their kiss from earlier, but she pushed it away.

"Your creativity center, as I said. I have a

certain…notoriety in this area. And a number of business contacts."

"From all those years of perfecting your golf game instead of working." She flushed. "Sorry. I shouldn't have said that."

"That's okay. It was, after all, in the *Lawford Times*."

"Sunday edition," she added, as if that gave the gossip column more credence.

"My reputation needs a little polish, as you can see."

"And you think marrying an upstanding citizen like me can give you that polish. You'll go play a few links, get my money and we'll call it even?"

"In a way, yes."

Daphne stared at him, still dumbfounded that he'd suggest something as outrageous as marrying him. He wasn't proposing a love match—he was proposing a business deal. It was the kind of crazy idea her mother would have considered, just for the fun of it, regardless of how the decision might have impacted her child. Daphne refused to follow that same path, to live her life in that chaotic triangle. "Mr. Matthews, if this is some kind

of joke or misguided way to make me feel
wanted after my boyfriend broke up with
me—"

"I assure you it's neither."

"Or some really crazy publicity stunt you're
hoping to pull off for your company—"

"That would be a bonus, but no, it's not my
main reason for asking."

"Then just what is your main reason?"

He paused, drawing in a breath, his gaze
going to some spot on the far wall. After a
moment, he swiveled his attention on her. A
pretty powerful thing, Carter Matthews's
undivided attention. It sent a shiver rock-
eting through Daphne's veins. "I need respectability. With my customers, my father
and most especially—" he drew in another
breath "—with myself."

"And you think marrying me will give you
that?" She pushed back her chair, then rose.
"I don't think so. In fact, I think you're crazy."

He gave her that grin again. "I believe I
already called you that first."

She refused to give in to the temptation of
that smile, the contagiousness of it. She
knew, from reading the papers, exactly what

kind of respectability Carter Matthews lacked. She was the wrong person to give him that. "I'm sorry, Mr. Matthews, but I can't help you. With this marriage thing or your business."

She turned to go, but he was out of his chair in an instant, a hand on her arm. "Wait. Let me explain."

"You mean, let you talk me into this crazy scheme. I don't think so. I don't need a husband."

"But you do need funding for your creativity center. And I can get you that if you marry me."

Her gaze narrowed. "In name only, you mean."

"Yes. And in a year, feel free to divorce me, calling me a worthless cad who had all the commitment ability of a flea in a dog pound."

She laughed. "That may be true."

"I know this sounds crazy and unexpected and a whole lot of other things," he went on. "But give it some thought. I can help you get your money, and you can help me restore my reputation."

She snorted. "You must really think I'm a miracle worker."

When he winced, she felt bad. There were days when it was better if she just kept her mouth shut.

"I realize my past is a well-known joke in this area," Carter said, his voice less friendly and more distant now. "I have seen how it's hurting my business, too, and I can't let that happen. Making TweedleDee Toys succeed is more important than ever before."

His gaze was earnest, his words holding that deep ring of truth. But still…

Marry him? She barely knew him. All she knew about Carter Matthews was what she had read in the paper and seen in the Breakup Basket. He was, in his own words, a cad, something verified a hundred times over in print.

"Fine, I'll help you with your company. In a client/coach relationship only. As for your other proposal, I would do anything to get this creativity center funded," Daphne said. "Anything but marry you."

CHAPTER FIVE

WELL, that had gone well.

Carter headed back to his office at TweedleDee Toys and contemplated a quick stop in an insane asylum. What had made him propose the idea of *marriage?*

If there was one thing Carter knew he couldn't do well, it was marry. His description of himself—and his lack of commitment abilities—was true. He'd never had a relationship that lasted longer than a golf season.

Something about Daphne Williams, however, had him thinking about doing more than a little golfing. Ever since that kiss, he'd been off-kilter, his thoughts traveling down paths they'd never journeyed before.

But then she'd rejected him with barely a thought. He wasn't used to rejection, especially from a woman. Rather than dissuade him, her refusal had increased Carter's interest.

"Mr. Matthews," Pearl said, coming up to him before he even entered the building, her gray hair still in its severe bun, a few stray tendrils the only evidence that she was stressed, "we have a problem."

"Another one?" Carter bit back a sigh. When didn't he have a problem here? For the thousandth time he wondered what Uncle Harry had been thinking—or drinking—when he'd left the toy company to his wayward nephew. "What now?"

A flicker of sympathy ran across Pearl's features before she shifted into all-business mode. "Toy Castle has canceled all outstanding orders with us. They were—" she dipped her head to look at the clipboard in her hands "—'unimpressed with our summer offerings.'"

Carter let out a curse. The last thing he needed right now was another mess. "They're fifty percent of our sales."

"Fifty-two percent," Pearl corrected. "Or rather, they *were* fifty-two percent."

"And I take it no miracles happened while I was out?"

"Not unless you count Paul thinking he saw Richard Nixon's face in his chicken salad."

Carter chuckled. "At least someone here believes in the impossible."

Pearl's countenance softened. She reached forward and laid a hand on his arm. "You can do this, Mr. Matthews. I think." As she turned to go back into the building, another wisp of gray hair escaped her bun.

A sure sign the bad news was just beginning.

Carter circumvented the front offices and headed into the cubicles that housed his toy designers. Two of them were hovered over a drafting board, the third was huddled in his gray cubicle, sketching ideas. The fourth, Paul, sat at the back of the room, staring intently at the plastic container that held his lunch.

"Quick meeting, guys," Carter said.

They headed over, taking seats around the table, looking about as interested in what Carter had to say as a bunch of preschoolers at a physics lecture. Jason Ritter leaned back in his chair, arms crossed over his chest. "Let me guess. More golf tips?"

Carter grimaced. He *had* called a meeting one day just to show off a new golf club. He'd thought he was building camaraderie. Instead it had seemed to do the opposite. "No, we need to talk business."

Lenny raised a skeptical brow. "Do you want me to go get Pearl?"

"No," Carter said through gritted teeth. When were these men ever going to have an ounce of respect for him?

Probably when the company showed a profit. Hell, even he'd have respect for himself then.

Carter cleared his throat. "We've lost the Toy Castle account because they were unimpressed with our summer catalog."

Jason sent Paul a glare. "I told you no one would want to buy your stupid toy fire hydrant."

Paul shot back a glare. "Just because you couldn't keep your dog off it during the real world test didn't mean it wouldn't work. I should have taken that poodle and—"

"Guys," Carter cut in, hoping to head off

yet another shouting match. Tensions in TweedleDee Toys were running high, with the four toy designers more often at each other's throats than at their desks. "We need to pull together. Come up with something that will bust us out of this slump."

"This isn't a slump," Mike said. "It's the tolling of the death knell." He held up two fingers, swinging an imaginary bell back and forth.

The other three snickered.

Carter ignored them, even though he heard the same ringing in his own ears. "To help with that, I've hired Creativity Masters to come in and provide a little boost in the—"

"We don't need anyone telling us how to be creative," Paul interrupted. "We've been creating for years, without any help from 'creativity experts.'" He flicked air quotes around the last two words.

Carter reached over, grabbed a Cemetery Kitty prototype off the bookshelf and held it up. The toy let out a low, strained yowl. "And your idea of creating is a zombie kitty?"

"Hey, paranormal stuff is hot," Paul said.

"Look at the TV shows, for Pete's sake. Kids love that crap."

"They love *live* animals, Paul. Not ones that look like former stars from a horror movie."

Paul raised his chin with a little jerk of superiority. "And you know this because…? I have *two* kids, Matthews. How many do you have?"

Carter scowled. He ought to fire Paul for his out-and-out disrespect—a mood that seemed to have spread through the company—but he needed every employee he could get right now. "I don't have any kids, Paul, but I know enough that dead animals don't sell and neither do superheroes who wield mops." He leaned forward, dropping the stuffed animal onto the center of the table. It landed with a hard, thick plunk and a half-grunt of protest from the mechanical voice box. The men eyed the lifeless toy, then Carter. "I pay you—all of you—to come up with toys that sell. Not to find fault with me, or my personal life."

"And you think this Creativity Blasters—"

"Masters," Carter corrected.

Paul shrugged, as if the word made no difference. "—this creativity group can teach us how to design better toys?"

"Frankly, yes. Quality and innovation have gone to hell here—" Carter saw Jason and Paul each bite back a retort "—and we need to do something to get it back. I expect you all to cooperate with Daphne. Or I'll find someone who will."

Then he turned on his heel, leaving behind a room as silent as the furry toy on the table. Carter strode into his office, shut the door and leaned against the hard oak. He flipped out his cell phone, punched in a memorized number, then waited for the pickup on the other end. "Tell me how you did it."

Cade, Carter's twin brother, chuckled. "Did what? Because if you're asking for help with a woman, there are just some things about you I don't want to know."

"No, not about a woman," Carter said, sinking into the leather chair behind his desk, "though I have a problem there, too."

"Let me guess. You have too many dates scheduled for Friday night and need some ideas so you can finesse the breaking of one more heart?" In the background, Cade's wife Melanie shouted a hello to her brother-in-law.

For a second, Carter felt a stab of envy. Cade had the whole American dream—the house with the white picket fence, a great wife, a wonderful daughter and a happy undertow to his voice.

Carter had always thought he was happy, dating who he wanted, maintaining no ties, keeping his distance from anything remotely resembling a church and a white dress. But lately, there'd been this weird nagging in the back of his mind that said he was missing out on something.

Yeah, a life outside this damned office. He needed to knock back a few beers with the guys down at Sullivan's Pub, meet a woman with no strings attached and put this place—and all its frustrations—behind him for a few days. That would set him straight again.

Even as the thought occurred to him, though, it sent a sinking feeling into his gut. He didn't want to be the playboy of the Midwest anymore.

He wanted to look on something with

pride. To have a life he could admire, a job he did well. It seemed, though, that the more he tried to climb that mountain, the more the mountain tried to shove him back into his place.

"Cade, I don't need your help with my dating life, never have, never will," Carter said, forcing a laugh into his voice, making himself sound like the same old confident Carter. "I just wanted to know how you managed to put in sixty thousand hours into a job you hated."

"I thought you were looking forward to stepping into Uncle Harry's shoes."

"I was. But it's a lot harder than I thought it would be."

Cade let out a sigh. "You don't want to hear my advice."

Carter rubbed at his temples, trying to ease the headache that seemed to have become a constant companion. "Yeah, I do."

"Stick with it. Ride out the storm. Pick your cliché, Carter, but just don't quit."

"And I'll be the better man for it," Carter said, echoing words he had heard from his father so many times in the last thirty-seven years that he might as well have had them fashioned into a bumper sticker.

Was it possible his father was right? Carter hated to admit it, but Jonathon's logic made a certain sense. When was the last time he'd stuck to anything that required more of a commitment than a lease?

Cade sighed. "Basically, yes. You've never worked hard for a thing in your life, Carter, and you know it."

Carter thought of the grades that had come easily, the investments that had paid themselves back with little more than guesswork on his part, the opportunities that had always seemed to be there when he needed one. All his life, it seemed as if he'd been in the right place at the right time.

Until now.

"Yeah, I do," Carter admitted. "But that was high school, Cade, not real life. I wasn't playing with people's jobs, their livelihoods. They depend on me here, to keep them employed. I can't just charm my way into a bunch of orders or smile at the guys and convince them to hang with me until I figure this out. I don't think this toy thing is a good fit for me. I mean, what the hell do I know about what kids want? What's fun?"

"Did you ever think that's the reason Uncle Harry left you the company instead of me?"

"Because he wants me to breed? Or get down on the floor with some baby dolls and a two-year-old?" Carter chuckled. "I don't think so. I'm the last man on earth who should be buying a three-bedroom ranch and having kids." If anything, Daphne's refusal of his proposal had hammered that point home.

"No, Carter," Cade said, his voice quieter now, filled with the concern of a brother, the subconscious knowledge of a twin who sometimes knew Carter better than he knew himself. "Uncle Harry left you the company because he wanted you to have fun. You never have, not really."

Carter shook his head. "Cade, I—"

"No, you haven't," his brother interrupted. "You've put on a good show, but I know and you know, it's all empty behind the curtain."

Carter didn't respond. Something thick and heavy had formed in his throat and he just shook his head, even though he knew

Cade couldn't see his disagreement. He crossed the room, sat in the leather chair that had been part of Uncle Harry's legacy and put his feet up on the desk.

But he felt far from relaxed.

"Carter, put the flashy cars and the golf and the women aside for a while," Cade said, his voice deep with concern and that twin knowledge that seemed to always read Carter's mind. "Make a go of this CEO thing. You might be surprised to find you're good at it *and* you enjoy it."

"All I do is live at work lately and it hasn't paid off at all. If anything, my being here makes it worse."

"Well, maybe that's going to be good for you."

Carter snorted. "You sound like Dad now. And the last thing I need is more of that."

"Just a little brotherly advice." Cade called out to Melanie that he'd be right there. "Anyway, we're having a barbecue tonight, if you want to come by and share a couple beers. I promise to shut up and not lecture you. It's the dad in me, makes me think I can tell everyone what to do."

Carter chuckled, his mood softened by Cade's words, even though they were a harsh truth he'd been avoiding. "Well, with such an attractive offer, how can I refuse?"

"See you at seven," Cade replied, his voice quiet with unvoiced concern and care. "Oh, and bring some potato salad so you can get me out of the doghouse for forgetting to buy some this morning."

Carter laughed, promised to stop by the store, then hung up. For a long while, he stayed where he was, replaying the conversation with his brother. Then the phone on his desk started ringing and the bad news flood began anew.

Cade was right. Carter did need to find some fun in his life.

And he knew just where to look.

CHAPTER SIX

"HE ASKED you to do what?" Reilly's eyes widened, nearly bugging out of his head. He scooted his chair closer to Daphne's, hanging on her every word.

"Marry him." Daphne scoffed, waving a hand in dismissal at the very idea. "He thinks if I became Mrs. Carter Matthews, corporations would be more inclined to give me money. The PR potential and all that, given that he's the darling of the gossip columns."

"Would you have a church wedding or just one of those quickie things?"

"Reilly, I'm *not* marrying a man because it would be good public relations. I'd like a real romance, with a guy who proposes because he actually loves me. You know, the whole white dress, church thing. And vows that are truly meant, not just created as part of a marketing scheme."

"I knew it!" Reilly grinned. "You're a closet romantic after all."

"Am not." But the protest was a weak one.

"Eloping can be romantic, too, you know."

She gaped at Reilly. "You don't seriously think I should do this, do you?"

"Yes, I do." He laid a hand on her arm, his voice softened by concern. "Listen, Daph, I've known you for a long time. I've been with you almost since the day you started this place. I think you're a genius at what you do, but when it comes to your personal life—"

"When it comes to my personal life, what?" she asked, when he didn't finish.

His face scrunched up with that look of honesty Daphne knew she didn't want to hear. "Well, sweetie, you're about as spontaneous as Old Faithful."

"I am not."

"Oh, yeah? Tell me one spontaneous thing you've done in, oh, say the last five years."

"There was the time I…" Daphne's voice trailed off, her mind coming up empty. "Oh, and the…" She shut her mouth again. Still nothing in the memory banks. "Well, there were plenty of things, I'm sure."

"No, there weren't. You keep telling people that spontaneity is the key to freeing their creativity and you—"

Daphne leaped to her feet, flinging out a finger to point at Reilly. "I bought that purple jacket at Macy's! On my lunch break. *And,* I paid full price."

Reilly cocked his head to look at her. "Honey, that is sad. I mean, really sad."

Daphne shifted on her feet. "It is, isn't it?"

"You need to loosen up, Daphne. Maybe if you do, you'll have as much fun outside the office as you do when you're here."

Reilly was right. Her work was fun and allowed her to express that outgoing side of herself that she usually tucked away before she went home. It was as if Daphne had divided herself into two people: creative Daphne who gave companies a new way to spark their imaginations and subdued Daphne, who didn't want to take any chances because she'd grown up in a home where chaos was as regular as fish on Fridays.

"I did do something spontaneous and

totally out of character. Today, in fact," she said to Reilly.

"Let me guess. You bought the matching skirt?"

"No." She toyed with the pencils in her "Fun People Make Fun Workers" coffee mug. "I kissed Carter Matthews in Lombardo's."

Reilly's jaw dropped for the second time in a half an hour. "You did? That's just so awesome, Daph. Exactly what the doctor ordered, if you ask me."

"No, it wasn't. It was a mistake. One I'm never going to make again."

"Why, was he bad?"

"At kissing?" Heat invaded Daphne's cheeks, flooding in with the memory of Carter Matthews's kiss. The very vivid memory of Carter. His body against hers. His lips working magic, the way he'd cupped her jaw and made her feel like the only woman in the world. "Oh, no. He wasn't bad. He was good. Very, *very* good."

"See, that's exactly what I'm talking about. You have your entire personal life down to a science, when what you really need is more kisses like that. Maybe even a couple of wedding bells." Reilly gave her a hopeful grin.

She shook her head. "It's supremely stupid to jump into a marriage because some guy wants to polish his playboy image. Carter Matthews can marry someone else to save his butt." And she could go on living the way she was. Maybe throw in an impromptu vacation here and there. Daphne didn't need to have any more spontaneity than that.

She'd learned long ago that acting irrationally painted you into a corner. She had her escape, in work. She didn't need that in her day-to-day life, no matter how exciting and amazing that kiss had been.

"So," Reilly said, "it's okay with you if Carter marries someone else *and* kisses someone else at the altar?"

As always, her assistant had gotten straight to the point. She'd hired Reilly for his ability to pinpoint exactly what the problem was with a client's business—and then create a plan to solve it. He wasn't supposed to do that with her, too.

Daphne turned away and busied herself

with straightening a pile of file folders that were already in alignment, trying not to think of Carter Matthews kissing someone else exactly the way he'd kissed her. She blocked the image of him smiling at another woman, touching another woman's face, body. "I don't care who else Carter Matthews kisses. Or marries, for that matter."

"Sure you don't," Reilly said, clearly not believing her at all. "So why don't you go out to dinner with him tonight and tell him so?"

"Will you quit, Reilly?" A gust of exasperation followed her words. "I am not going out to dinner with him. I'm going home, popping a Lean Cuisine into the microwave and watching that episode of *ER* I taped when I was out of town last week."

Reilly smiled the secretive smile that told Daphne he'd been matchmaking again. "Sorry, but you have other dinner plans. Not to mention, much better plans than some overprocessed, frozen rubber chicken. Carter called a few minutes ago. It took some doing but I managed to get him to tell me that he was calling to ask you to dinner. I took the liberty of telling him you were free tonight."

"You did what?"

"I offered to make reservations at Chez Amore, but he said he already had a dinner plan for the two of you," Reilly went on, ignoring her, "and he told me to tell you to dress casual. I think, though, that if you want to knock him off his feet, you should wear that black dress you wore to the Chamber of Commerce Casino Night last year. You know, the dress with the—"

"You set up a date for me? Without asking me?"

"Yes, I did." Reilly gave her a supremely satisfied smile. "You need a break and you know it. You also need a man who has more ambition than mastering some blood and guts game. Not to mention, you like this Carter Matthews." He put up a hand to cut off her ready protest. "For Pete's sake, Daphne, it's written all over your face. Particularly in the way you blushed when you talked about him kissing you. Now, stop being such a nitwit and go to dinner with him."

She parked a fist on her hip. "Hey, who's the boss here?"

"Me, at least in what's good for you. I've

come to an executive decision," he said, raising his chin a notch in superiority. "You are no longer CEO of your personal life, Daphne Williams. You're *fired*." He made the hand gesture made famous by Donald Trump, then laughed. "I've always wanted to do that."

Reilly walked back to his desk, humming another love song. Daphne hated to admit it, but Reilly was right. She did need a new life manager. Someone who could help her find a balance between stability and fun.

Reilly, however, saw marriage as the fastest route to change. Daphne had no intentions of taking that particular highway.

"Tell me you don't have a dog and two kids waiting for me behind door number one," Daphne said three hours later, sitting in Carter's Lexus in the driveway of a well-kept home on the outskirts of Lawford. A midsize Tudor with a stone front, the house was impressive without being overwhelming.

Carter laughed. He grabbed the container of potato salad on the seat, with its little Made By sticker from the nearby grocery on top. "No, this is my brother's house. The only menacing thing waiting behind that door, besides Cade and Melanie, is Grover."

Carter got out of the car and came around to open her door, but Daphne beat him to it. She didn't need chivalry—regardless of what Reilly thought.

"Grover?"

"He means well," Carter said, grinning at her as they walked up the red brick path that led to the front door. "Just watch his tongue."

Before they had reached the top step, the front door was opened by a petite brown-haired woman with a welcoming smile and laughing green eyes. Undoubtedly this was Melanie, Cade's wife. "Carter! You didn't tell me you were bringing a—"

A massive ball of gray and white fur came scooting past her, down the stairs and straight into Daphne. He leaped up, paws against her chest, and started licking.

"Meet Grover," Carter said, laughing, reaching for the dog's collar, trying to tug him off. Daphne wobbled a little under the canine poundage.

"Oh God, I'm so sorry about him."

Melanie hurried forward, tugging the dog down by his collar and giving him a few stern corrections. "He has absolutely no manners."

"Much like my brother." A man who could have been Carter's double exited the house and loped down the stairs. He clapped Carter on the shoulder and gave him a grin.

Carter chuckled, then gestured between Daphne and his brother. "Daphne, meet Cade, my twin in everything but personality."

"Yeah, it's too bad I got all the personality and you got the leftovers." Cade grinned, then gave his brother a good-natured jab in the shoulder. Carter sparred with his brother, the two of them joking about who had come first and who had the better looks.

Daphne's heart constricted. The obvious love between the two, the camaraderie that had now expanded to include Melanie—to serve as judge in their verbal joust—was nearly painful to watch.

Daphne shrugged it off. She'd been alone nearly all her life. Watching a family interact had never set her off before—and it wasn't going to now. "I'm Daphne," she said, extending her hand and introducing herself before Carter could.

"Cade Matthews," Carter's brother said. He opened his arm to indicate his wife. "And this is my wife, Melanie."

A quick look passed between the couple, the kind that spoke of merry Christmases and late night snuggling. Once again, the band wrapped around Daphne's chest.

"Some might say she's his better half," Carter whispered in Daphne's ear, his breath warm and enticing along her neck.

Introductions complete and Grover distracted by a rubber toy that Melanie produced from somewhere on the porch, the four of them moved through the house and out to the backyard. Tendrils of smoke drifted off the grill, scented with hickory and maple. The freshly cut grass, lush and thick, created an oasis setting in the large backyard. In the left corner, a white wooden swing sat beneath a blooming crabapple tree. "This is gorgeous," Daphne said to Melanie. "I don't get this kind of view from my apartment, that's for sure."

"Thanks," Melanie said, handing her an

icy margarita in a glass decorated with cacti and sombreros. "We sold our Indianapolis house last year to live closer to the coffee shop and our daughter, Emmie. She's going to Lawford U. Graduates in a year and a half." Melanie laughed. "Gosh, that makes me sound ancient. The mother of a college graduate."

It all seemed so perfect, so ideal, Daphne wanted to reach out a grab a taste of their life for herself. How many years had she wished for this very thing? For a house—no, a *home*—a yard, a dog? A mother who bragged about her, a father who joined in the chorus?

And most of all, a man who looked at her the way Cade looked at Melanie?

She turned and caught Carter's eye. He grinned at her, and her heart flipped over. Which was crazy. She barely knew the man.

But as she sipped her margarita and answered Cade's question about how she took her steak, she wondered if maybe Reilly had been right. Half her problem all along—

Was spending too much damned time planning and analyzing instead of just jumping in.

* * *

An hour later, after the last corn cob was consumed—the honors going to Cade after he won an impromptu trivia game against his brother, showing the men still retained a bit of the boys they had been, and the final bits of steak were scarfed up by Grover, Carter and Daphne wandered the yard, pausing to smell some flowers, admire the newly installed garden beds, before finally stopping at the swing.

He pushed off with his heel, sending them on a gentle sway over the green lawn carpet. "Thank you."

"For what?"

"For coming. I enjoyed having you here with me tonight." He grinned. "Particularly to run interference with Cade."

She laughed, then smoothed the edge of her skirt against the white planks. "I was going to say the same thing to you. I haven't been at a family type thing in a… Well, a long time."

"Really? What about your folks?"

"Distant." Physically and emotionally, but Daphne didn't add that. There was no reason to go into her childhood sob story. It was done, over and unchangeable. "My grandparents were the ones to hold this kind of thing, but they lived in Maine so I only saw them once or twice a year. My grandfather died when I was twelve. My grandmother really went downhill after that. They'd been together all their lives and I guess she never adjusted to life without him. She lived in a nursing home in Arizona for several years until she died. My mother and stepfather live in Arizona, too—when they're not globe-trotting."

"Do you have brothers and sisters?"

She shook her head.

"Not even any cousins to taunt you?"

"My dad died when I was little. After that, my mother started marrying one man after the other, as if she was trying to get the whole thing perfect. The one thing she didn't do with any of her husbands was have more kids."

"Sounds like we have a few things in common," Carter said, toeing at the grass as the swing glided back and forth. "My mother left us when Cade and I were little boys—"

"Oh, Carter, I'm sorry," Daphne said, laying a hand on his.

Carter looked down at her delicate palm clasping his much larger one, and something that had long ago hardened in his heart began to soften. He'd spent most of his life doing his best not to remember that day and then, wham, here it was, raising its ugly head. Yet, with Daphne's caring touch and her soft voice, it seemed to make it all okay somehow.

"I'm a grown-up," he said. "I'm fine with it now."

"Yeah, that's exactly how I feel about my childhood." She didn't say anything further and he got the feeling she enjoyed talking about her younger years as much as he did—which meant not at all. "So," she said, her tone taking on that higher pitch that signaled a change in conversational direction, "what made you decide to run the toy company? Couldn't you have just hired a CEO after your uncle left it to you?"

He grinned. "I take it I don't strike you as the toy type."

A smile played across her lips, dappled

by the end-of-day sunlight peeking through the leaves of the tree above them. "More the Porsche dealership type."

"Now *that* I probably would have been good at." He pushed the swing a little harder, bringing a breeze whispering over them. "Believe me, no one was more shocked than I was when Uncle Harry left me the company."

"Because of your reputation." The words were said without malice, with the tinge of honesty.

"Yeah. Failure was, after all, what my father expected of me."

"And you decided you weren't going to do that anymore?" Daphne said.

"I've been a 'disappointment'—" Carter put air quotes around the word "—all my life. What better way to annoy my father than to actually succeed at something?"

Daphne's light laughter was tinged with tones of understanding. "And that's why it's so important that you turn this business around?"

"That was what I wanted at first—just to prove the old man wrong—but then, after I spent time at TweedleDee, I realized something." He paused the swing and turned to look at her. "Those people—the employees—are depending on me. They need their jobs to pay their mortgage, raise their kids, feed their families."

"It's an awesome responsibility, isn't it?"

In that moment, a détente arose between them, a connection that tethered Carter to Daphne in a way he'd never been connected to a woman before. They shared a common language; similar worries. She understood him—

Something no one had ever done before.

"What about you?" he asked, the swing stopping as he turned to face her, putting the whole connection thing to the side for now. "Why did you become a creativity coach? Instead of a Porsche salesperson?"

She laughed a little, then shrugged, and he got the feeling that getting personal wasn't something Daphne liked to do. Then she drew in a breath, pushed off the swing, waiting for it to creak to and fro for a moment before she spoke. "My mother has never been the kind of person to stick to anything for very long. A town, a husband, a house. She likes change—a little too much."

"And that spawned your love of creativity?"

Sharp notes sounded in Daphne's laugh. "No, not at all. If anything, it made me want stability. But when I'd spend summers with my grandfather, it was like heaven. I loved having fun, but then, as I grew up, I wanted to use that fun in smart ways."

"To help businesses."

She nodded.

"What about personal fun?"

"That I don't have," she said. "No time. No inclination for messy relationships."

"And yet, here you are, sitting with a man who's made personal fun his middle name. Maybe there's something I can teach you." He grinned.

Something akin to fear flickered in her eyes. Did the thought of cutting loose, of stepping out of her comfort zone, scare the woman who made her living teaching others that spontaneity was a good tool?

"Anyway," she said, dismissing the subject, "I'd been looking for a space to create a similar environment for kids, but my budget wasn't big. The lot on Prince became available six months ago, and I bought it, using up all my reserve cash, hoping to get a donor for the rest. But if I don't, I'll find a way to build it either way."

"To make sure every child has a Grandfather Wallace."

Tears shimmered in her eyes, but she washed them away with another smile. "Yes, at least every child in the southern Indiana area."

He sat back against the seat, enjoying the slow pendulum movement of the wooden seat, and the view of Daphne Williams. Maybe he'd been meeting the wrong women or maybe he'd never had a conversation more meaningful than deciding between the crème brûlée and the cheesecake, but Daphne had intrigued him. Multiple dimensions made up this woman, sparking his curiosity. "I think that's really wonderful."

She shrugged the compliment off. "It may be a total flop."

He shook his head. "I doubt it, not with you running it."

"Thanks."

The swing rocked them gently, swaying

with the breeze. "Speaking of spontaneity, I wanted to apologize. That marriage idea was either a moment of craziness or a drop in my blood sugar."

They shared a laugh, but a part of Carter wondered what would happen if she had said yes.

"I'll help you get the funding," he said, wanting only to see her smile again, to hear her laughter, "no strings attached."

"Really?"

He nodded.

"Oh, thank you, Carter." She put a hand on his, her gaze catching his, and in those blue depths, he saw a flicker of vulnerability. It scared him as much as it drew him closer. This was a woman he could hurt—

And that was the one thing Carter didn't want to do.

"Daphne," he began, trying to find a way to corral the confusing jumble of emotions inside him, to tell her he wanted more—and yet, at the same time, that he wasn't sure he was even capable of that. "I—"

Before he could finish, Grover bounded onto his lap, muddy paws speckling a pattern across Carter's pants. The dog scrambled into the seat, his tail smacking Daphne in the face, his front feet pouncing all over Carter. He panted and let out a bark, then settled in between them.

Or as well as a dog that weighed more than a ten-year-old could settle.

"What were you going to say?" Daphne asked, her hand on Grover's head, clearly not bothered by the disruption. Her eyes were clear, guileless.

Trusting him.

Carter returned his regular, noncommittal smile to his face. A woman like Daphne Williams deserved better than him. "Someone clearly has a crush on you," Carter said.

She drew in a breath, her gaze on his. "Who would that be?"

Carter planted the grin that had broken a hundred hearts onto his face. "Grover, of course."

This time, though, as Daphne laughed and nuzzled the dog's giant head, something broke inside of Carter's heart.

CHAPTER SEVEN

EVER since Daphne had arrived at Tweedle-Dee Toys this morning to begin her first creativity exercise, Carter had kept things business-only. As much as he wanted to revisit those moments on the swing, he knew it was a temporary state.

A shiny new toy, as his father called it. Soon as the commitment noose began tightening around Carter, he had no doubt he'd be out of Daphne's life.

Uh-huh. That was exactly why he'd proposed to her. Because he wanted *less* commitment. He'd clearly been around too much plastic lately.

Now she stood in the center of the design offices, commanding the attention of every male pair of eyes, particularly Carter's. He watched her speak, running through a bio and a quick info-bite about her company. Her movements were fluid, in tune with her melodic voice. "So, are you ready?" she asked the four designers.

Though they looked a little befuddled, the four men seated at the table nodded.

"Great." She turned to Carter. "That means you, too."

"Me?" He directed a hand toward the designers. "You don't need me. Those are the guys who make the magic happen."

Lately, though, their magic had been more along the lines of the kind in a backyard magic show, complete with the Dixie cups and a pom-pom.

"You can join in later," Daphne said, making it clear he wouldn't escape the training. She turned her attention back to the men. "Let's get started with an easy exercise first." Daphne dug in her bag and pulled out a board game, then laid it on the table.

"Chutes and Ladders?" Mike said. "Are you kidding me?"

"Part of your target audience is playing this," Daphne explained. "It's one of the top selling games in the country and has been for decades. What we want to know is why and how you can take what we learn here and translate it into sales of your own toys."

She handed out the plastic people-shaped pieces, with each of the four designers taking a color. They started playing, with little enthusiasm at first. But when Paul hit the chute that sent him back to Start and another designer edged closer to the ending square, the competition heated up. "You're not going to win," Paul said, flicking the multicolored spinner. "I'm a master at this game."

Mike arched a brow. "Play much in your spare time?"

"Hey, I have kids," Paul said. "I, ah, have to keep them entertained somehow."

Carter stood to the side, glad there were only four pieces, and also glad Daphne had tried this. What had at first seemed like a silly idea to him had brought out the kid in his toy designers. When Mike captured the win, Daphne moved them on to a set of army men. A mock battle for control of the laminate tabletop ensued, pitting two against two.

"Here," Daphne said, coming up beside

him. He inhaled, and with the breath, caught the scent of her perfume, sweet and delicate. "You can be the invading general." She dumped a pile of tiny green men into his palms.

"What? No. Really, I'm not—"

"Part of getting your team energized is you becoming part of the team," she said. "Use these to outflank Paul. He thinks he's got the tabletop all sewn up."

Carter looked down at the plastic pieces. The offices of TweedleDee Toys faded out of his vision.

His memory reached back. He saw Cade, and him. Army men set up in a pile of dirt in the backyard. Imaginary borders drawn with a stick. There'd been battles and burials, maneuvers and mock medals.

Then, their mother striding by, a suitcase in one hand and the keys to the station wagon in the other. A quick kiss on each boy's head, then she was gone, pulling out of the driveway so fast, the rear wheel streaked a dent in the grass. It had taken three years before the lawn healed.

And a lot longer for the rest of them.

"I don't have time for this foolishness," Carter said, dumping the army men onto the table. The four men paused in their game of world domination to gape at him. Carter turned and left the room, shutting the door on the fake war and most of all, on memories that hadn't been erased with a little extra fertilizer and grass seed.

Daphne found Carter in his office an hour later. Carter never returned, never even popped in to check on their progress. After the design team was done and back at work, Daphne packed up the toys and games. On the floor, she spotted one lone army man. She picked it up, turning it over in her palm, recalling Carter's reaction.

The hard plastic cut into her palm as she closed her hand around it, then stuffed it into the front pocket of her bag.

Daphne headed down the hall toward Carter's office. The open door allowed a peek of him at work, head bent over the desk, a scowl on his face as he ran some numbers through an adding machine and apparently didn't get the total he was hoping for.

She knocked lightly on the door. He looked up at her, blue eyes connecting and sending a shiver through her veins. "Daphne." Her given name rolled off his tongue in a quiet baritone.

"We're, ah, all done in there." She thumbed in the direction of the designers' offices.

"How'd it go?"

"Great. We played a few games, then did some brainstorming exercises. By the time I left, they were nearly shouting over each other, throwing out new ideas, scribbling sketches on the whiteboard."

"Good," Carter said.

"After the retreat, we'll really be able to capitalize on the team building. You won't even recognize them."

"Thank you, Daphne. I appreciate all you've done."

A smile slipped across her lips. "My pleasure."

For a moment, he watched her, until her smile faltered and the heat of awareness charged through her body. Then Carter rose, skirted his desk and came to a stop a few inches away from her. "I do believe I owe you something in return."

Her mind whispered that he meant to kiss her—and everything within her went still at the thought. Carter Matthews may be bad for her in a hundred different ways, but he was oh-so-good in kissing her.

"Here," he said, putting a business card into her palm. "I had an early golf game with James Klein, who owns a chain of jewelry stores. He's excited about the creativity center and intends to pony up twenty thousand dollars. Tomorrow, I'm meeting with Dave Jenkins, who owns that home building company. You know, the one that wins all the awards for unique designs? I figure he'll want in on this, too."

"That's great," she replied, closing her hand over the card, glancing down at it so the disappointment wouldn't show on her face. "Thanks."

"My pleasure," he said, echoing her words.

She glanced up at him again. Their gazes caught. Daphne's heart began to beat faster than it ever had before, anticipation stirring inside her even as she knew it was crazy to get involved with this man. He treated his company, and his relationships, with a cavalier air.

She wanted someone serious. Someone dependable. Someone about as exciting as a Labrador retriever. Someone who didn't come readily equipped with the very chaos she had tried to escape.

"I better get back to the office," she said, but didn't leave. Didn't grab her purse, or her jacket, because the only thing she really wanted to grab right now was standing right in front of her.

"I should get back to work, too," Carter said, his gaze never leaving hers. Desire twisted inside Daphne, curling its tense grip around her willpower, rooting her to the spot.

Carter took a half step forward, then lifted his hand to her chin, sending warmth skating along her skin. His thumb traced along her jawline, releasing a shiver down her spine. "I'm going to kiss you," he said, his voice low and gruff. "Is that all right?"

That was more than all right. She nodded, mute. Waiting, wanting and needing.

Then, finally, he leaned down, brushing his lips across hers, a taste instead of a bite. Her body quieted, anticipation catching her breath and holding it hostage.

Carter drew back and in his gaze she saw something dark and deep.

Raw, hungry need.

She swallowed, thinking she should leave. Back away, walk out the door, before she got tangled up in the very thing she'd spent a lifetime avoiding.

But her feet didn't move. Instead she opened her mouth, closed the distance between them and kissed him back.

Kissing Carter Matthews—or rather, being kissed by Carter Matthews—was unlike any other kiss she'd ever experienced. Music hummed between them, set to a jazzy beat, a pace set by him and matched by her. His hands cradled her head, tangling in her hair. Against her, his chest was hard, secure. She wondered wildly what he looked like beneath the tie, the button-down shirt, the neatly pressed gray trousers.

What he did with his mouth sent Daphne nearly over the edge. He didn't just kiss her, he treasured her, his mouth an urgent, heated caress. She reached around his back, drawing him closer, forgetting her resolve to stay away from a man who went through women the same way some people went through a cookie jar.

Because right this minute, he didn't make her feel like one more chocolate chip in the bag. Every ounce of his touch whispered that she was a rarity, a one-of-a-kind. The only woman he wanted.

Someone knocked on his door—a door Daphne realized belatedly they had forgotten to close—then cleared their throat. Daphne and Carter broke apart, her face flushed and hot, her body screaming disappointment.

"Mr. Matthews, may I have a moment?" A severe-looking woman with a gray bun stepped into his office, her face devoid of expression. "Just one minute and then you can get back to your—" she looked between the two of them "—meeting."

"Uh, certainly, Pearl. Pearl Jenkins, this is Daphne Williams. She's the creativity coach I hired for TweedleDee Toys."

To Daphne's surprise, the woman passed

up the chance to comment on the whole idea of creativity and being caught kissing the boss. Instead she shook hands with Daphne, then headed to Carter's desk, spreading a sheaf of papers across the gleaming surface. "We need to have a—" she glanced again at Daphne "—financial discussion."

Carter scowled. Clearly this wasn't his favorite topic.

Daphne well remembered those frustrating early days before she had a few regular clients and dependable income. Even now, Creativity Masters had the occasional run of cash flow issues, and she'd start worrying once again about where to cut and what to save. Then, things would pick up, and she'd worry about meeting the demand. Either way, it all meant long hours and a constant burden of worry. Being the owner wasn't nearly as glamorous as it looked.

Daphne turned, grabbing her coat off the chair and her purse from the floor. "You're busy. We can talk later," she said to Carter.

"You don't have to go, Daphne. I'll be done in a minute."

"No, I do," she said, sucking in some of

the willpower that had deserted her earlier. If Pearl hadn't come in and interrupted them, she knew she'd have traveled down a thought path that could only lead to disaster. Carter was completely the wrong man for her. He was a playboy, a dabbler. And worst of all, the kind of loose cannon she didn't need in her life. "I have priorities and so do you. It'd be best if we remembered those."

Then she turned and left, before her hormones outflanked her better judgment.

CHAPTER EIGHT

"HE KISSES you *and* he comes up with a good chunk of the funding so you can break ground," Kim said the next night, camped on Daphne's sofa with a pile of rented chick flicks and an extra large pepperoni pizza. "I'm sorry, Ducky, but I'm not seeing a downside to Carter Matthews."

Daphne slipped the first of the movies into the DVD player, then returned to the couch. Her gaze went to the ceiling, knowing that Carter was only a couple of floors above her. She'd seen his car in the parking lot; she knew he was home. All it would take would be a journey of two flights to be with him again. She settled further into the sofa, cementing her resolve to stay away from the playboy who spelled nothing but heartbreak, even if he'd schmoozed enough people that she had all but thirty thousand of the money she needed for the creativity center. Carter Matthews had pulled off a miracle, but that didn't mean he was good boyfriend material. "You know his reputation, Kim. I'd be just another notch on his bedpost."

"Maybe not. Look at Warren Beatty. Hugh Hefner. They got married."

"Hugh *Hefner?*"

Kim laughed. "Okay, he's not the best example. But you get the idea."

"I'm not looking for a husband or a relationship. Particularly not now. Groundbreaking is in less than two weeks, then I'll be busy overseeing the construction, talking with the investors—"

"And avoiding the subject of Carter."

Daphne nodded. "That's the plan."

"Are you insane?" Kim asked. "He's hot, he's well-off and he's crazy about you. What's not to like?"

"You don't understand. When I kissed him, I…" She paused. "I liked it."

"Duh. That's what's supposed to happen."

"You don't understand. It's different for

me, Kim. I…" She drew in a breath. "I just don't do that."

"I know, Ducky. But maybe a little change is in order, before you get stuck."

"Maybe," Daphne said. Why did everyone in her life think that—except for Daphne? She rose and went into the kitchen for a refill of soda. On her way back, she spotted her mail, the pile untouched since she'd come home, her brain all muddled by a certain handsome bachelor.

A bright yellow envelope caught her eye. She shoved the bills aside and pulled it out. Return address: England.

Kim joined her. "A card from Carter?"

"No. A letter from my mom." Surprise raised the register of her voice. How long had it been? Two years at least, and even so, hope raised inside her, as if everything could change in one letter.

Kim's face softened in an understanding that came from years of seeing Daphne's hopes dashed, of watching Mary Williams breeze in and out of her life as flittingly as a summer shower. Daphne headed into the kitchen and returned with the Bacardi, splashing a bit of rum into Daphne's glass. "I think you might need that."

Daphne thanked Kim, but didn't take a sip. She slid her finger under the flap and opened the envelope. Inside, she found a two-page letter written on watermarked paper in her mother's familiar tight script.

Daphne scanned the letter, skipping over the breezy descriptions of life across the pond, as her mother called it, the excited recounts of museum tours and drives through the English countryside.

"I haven't heard from her in two years and here she starts out with a travelogue, as if we chatted on the phone last week?" Daphne shook her head. "I don't know why I expected anything different. That's the way my mother is."

Kim's hand rested on Daphne's shoulder. "You sure you want to read this now?"

Daphne nodded and flipped the first page over. At the top of the second page, her mother finally got to the point of her letter.

"Need you here…Brad's not doing well… can't handle this without you."

Disappointment plummeted like a stone

into her gut. Her mother was only writing because she needed Daphne's help. Not because she wanted to hang around long enough to actually be a part of Daphne's life. "My stepdad is sick and she's in a panic," Daphne told Kim. "She wants me to fly over there, help her with everything."

"Help her with what? Isn't he in a hospital?"

"You know my mother, Kim. She can't handle the details of life. The talks with the doctor, the dispensing of medicine, heck, the grocery shopping. Frankly I'm surprised she's still there and she hasn't run away yet."

"Like she did when you got sick," Kim said softly.

"Yeah." Daphne shook off the melancholy that had settled around her shoulders and put the letter aside. "Let's get back to those movies. I could use a few laughs tonight."

"You got it," Kim said, following Daphne back to the sofa and handing her friend the remote. "The rest can wait."

But Daphne didn't pay attention to the films playing on her television. She didn't watch the adventures of mismatched romance, the replays of classic plots with modern settings. Instead she sat on the sofa, the screen flickering in her eyes, and tried to decide, as she had so many times before, between duty and dreams.

Carter sat back in his chair and watched the frantic sketching of his toy designers, astonished at the change in thinking. Daphne Williams truly was a miracle worker.

And a whole lot more. The minute her name came to mind, it whispered up the memories of kissing her. Of how she insisted on resisting him at the same time she returned his kiss.

She'd come by this morning, and given the men the one game they could all work on together—a challenge to design a golf course. "You're the expert on golf," Mike said, waving Carter over to take the place of Lenny, who had a doctor's appointment that morning. "You better be on our team."

Daphne had left a gift certificate to a local sporting goods shop as the prize for the most unusual and creative design. That carrot had set the men to work, broken into two teams. They'd spent a fun hour sketching and erasing, before digging into the polymer clay and creating a 3-D version. When Daphne returned, and proclaimed Carter and Mike's design the best, the four men had a golf-off with a tiny ball and a popsicle stick to determine the ultimate winner.

It had been fun. More fun than Carter could remember having in years. He'd given Daphne a grateful thank-you as she headed out the door to her next appointment. When he'd returned to the design offices, the men had been hard at work, laughing and working together.

Carter stood there for a good five minutes in stunned surprise. Then the men had rushed over with their ideas. He'd given the go-ahead on two of the designers' new ideas: a geography board game that incorporated a search for buried treasure and a travel puzzle that had kids navigating a silver ball up a stack of ladders to increase their points and reach the end. The designers eagerly went back to work, fine-tuning their projects.

"Mr. Matthews, you have a visitor waiting in your office." Kelly, the receptionist, gave him a bright, did-I-do-the-right-thing smile.

A temp from Reliable Staffing, sent to replace the ill Sara, Kelly had been gunning for a permanent position at TweedleDee ever since they'd sent her over. She'd yet to master the phone system or the little pink "While You Were Out" slips, which didn't bode well for her potential at TweedleDee.

"Who is it?" Carter asked.

"Oh, gee. I didn't think to ask." Kelly's face fell. "Do you want me to go in there and find out?"

She looked so stricken, Carter shook his head. "No, but please do next time."

"Okay. Sure thing." She jotted down a line or two on the slim yellow pad beside her. He could see it was filled with notes about everything from where the light switch was located to the best way to file phone messages. Carter gave her a sympathetic smile. He knew what it felt like to be totally out of your element.

He opened his office door, hoping he'd see Daphne's incredible legs and even prettier smile. Instead he saw a familiar gray pin-striped suit. "Dad. Twice in one week. That's got to be a record."

His father scowled at him. "Jerry Lawson called me yesterday."

Carter slipped behind his desk, folded his hands together and waited for the scolding that was sure to come. It felt odd to be on this side of the desk, when more often than not Carter had been the one in the visitor's chairs, taking a verbal beating from his father. "What did I do now?"

"He said you talked to him about supporting some kind of center."

Carter gave a quick nod. "That's not a crime."

"I didn't say it was." His father shook his head. "Why is every conversation with you an argument?"

"Because all you ever do is find fault with me."

"I do not."

Carter arched a brow in disagreement.

"Anyway," his father said on a gust, "I just wanted to…well, commend you." The word came out strangled and tight.

Carter leaned back in his chair, surprised. "Commend me?"

"Jerry said he was impressed with your

business knowledge. Thought this center thing was a nice thing to support, too. Tied in nice with what you're doing with this place." He gestured around the room, indicating the toy company.

For a moment, Carter sat there speechless, stunned by the unexpected praise. "Thank you."

"Don't get ahead of yourself." His father slapped that day's paper onto Carter's desk, the disapproval returned to its permanent place on his face. The moment, if there'd even been one, had passed. "Your escapades have once again made the front page."

Carter glanced down and saw a picture of him and Daphne entering Lombardo's. Gloria the gossip columnist had written a little teaser, wondering if Carter was "playing" with Daphne's emotions, a ha-ha pun on his toy company ownership. "That wasn't an escapade. It was a meeting."

His father flipped open the paper, revealing a second photo of Daphne and Carter kissing. "I've never had a meeting end like that."

Carter cursed under his breath. "Why won't they leave me alone?"

"Because you're the closest thing we have to news in Indiana. I had hoped that by this age, you would have learned to behave yourself in public."

Carter slammed the paper down. "And I would have hoped that by now you'd know me well enough to stop taking the media's word over your son's."

"You don't understand. I can't abide this." His father tapped at the paper.

"What you mean is you can't abide an imperfection. Not in yourself and especially not in your sons." Carter rose, placed his hands on the desk and faced his father. "I have news for you, Dad. None of us are perfect and we never will be. And what I can't abide is a father who has nothing but distaste for me. I'm sorry I don't measure up and that I'll never be what you wanted."

Carter turned and strode out of his office, leaving his father and the words he should have said years ago, behind.

When the plane landed in Portland, Maine, Carter had already decided this retreat was a huge mistake. For one, any euphoria from the earlier team building exercises had disappeared, and his toy designers were nothing but grumpy about the thought of being away from their homes for two days. They had hardly exchanged more than four words with him over the course of the trip, preferring to engross themselves in books, MP3 players and crossword puzzles.

He grabbed his bag out of the overhead compartment, then strode off the plane, the design staff forming their own little quartet behind him, the line so clearly delineated between them and him, it might as well have been neon-yellow. Just when Carter thought he was making headway—he ended up blazing a path in the wrong direction.

Daphne was waiting for them, standing behind the barrier of the security screening area. She had on a turquoise print skirt and dark brown kitten heels that emphasized her legs. His gaze traveled upward, past the dark brown sweater, to her eyes, wide and inquisitive behind her trademark glasses.

His heart flipped over in his chest, the feeling so odd, Carter stopped dead in his tracks, colliding with the man behind him.

"Did you see a stop sign here?" Paul grumbled.

Carter started forward, never losing eye contact with Daphne. Everything within him was centered on her, and multiplying with every step. Until he'd seen her, he hadn't realized how much he'd missed her in the last two days. It was as if he'd lost a limb and just now found it again. "Hi."

"You made it," Daphne said when the men reached her, offering the group a friendly smile, sending an insane twinge of jealousy through Carter that her smile had to be shared. "Reilly, my assistant, is already back at the house, getting our first exercises ready." She turned and the men fell into step around her, like an entourage. "So I hope you don't plan on relaxing because we'll be working. Only, this will be fun work, I promise."

The men cast her dubious glances, but followed nevertheless. She led them out of the airport and into a van she'd had parked outside. Paul climbed in the passenger's seat, leaving Carter in the middle seat with the other three men crammed into the far back, the camaraderie created by the golf exercise gone. The drive to the house in Boothbay Harbor went fast, as they left the suburbia of Portland and headed toward the coastline. They wound through Boothbay Harbor and then down a tree-covered street, the neighborhoods dropping away, the woods crowding in as they climbed a steep hill set back from civilization. Finally they came to a stop in front of a multigabled house with a huge wraparound porch, all of it grayed by the ocean air. Behind the house, a small white sailboat bobbed in the sparkling water. A hammock and a pair of Adirondack chairs beckoned from the grassy area, welcoming them as easily as a Norman Rockwell painting. Palladian windows faced the water, reflecting glints of blue and green like stained glass.

"This is an incredible place," Carter said as they all climbed out of the van, retrieving their luggage from the back.

"Thanks. It used to be my grandparents' house. I inherited it when my grandmother passed away." The men murmured their appreciation for the environment, pausing to inhale the unfamiliar ocean air, before heading inside.

The next few minutes were spent choosing bedrooms, with the designers opting to room together over rooming with Carter. Daphne took the master bedroom, Reilly bunked with Carter. Disappointment sunk inside him, but maybe he'd get lucky and Reilly would provide a few secrets to winning Daphne's heart.

Win her heart? What was he thinking? He was here to save his company, not build on what they had started in the restaurant. Heck, what had been building every time he looked at her.

Yet, a part of him wondered if it would be possible to have both—success and Daphne.

"We'll have something to eat then get right to work," Daphne said, her focus still on the team and the job at hand. Carter would do well to learn from her example. She opened the fridge and pulled out several ready-made platters of cold cuts, vegetables and fruits.

"You did all this?" he said.

She laughed. "I can do a lot of things, but

cook isn't one of them. I ordered them from the local deli."

Carter barely ate. Instead he watched Daphne joke with the men, make her way around the table, getting to know each of them with her light, easy touch. They gravitated toward her, clearly at ease. Carter could see why. Everything about Daphne—her gestures, her voice—had an animated, lively air. She welcomed people into her world as easily as sunshine.

Witty and smart, she matched Carter in conversation and intelligence. She intrigued him and invaded his thoughts more often than not.

When their appetites were sated, Daphne cleared the dishes, then faced the men, her back against the laminate countertop. "While we were at the airport, Reilly set up our first creativity exercise. It's a treasure hunt—of sorts." Daphne pushed off from the counter, then handed sheets of paper to each of the five men. "You'll split into two teams, then find these seven items, all hidden in the woods around here."

Paul ran a finger down the list. "How's

this supposed to make us more creative? I mean, finding a *clock?* A teddy bear?"

"For one, it builds teamwork. And for another, these items are hidden in some very unusual places. Trust me, you won't think to look for a salad bowl in the kind of place Reilly hides it." She grinned at the men. Reilly echoed her smile. "The first team to come back with all seven items gets first dibs on tomorrow's task, or if you'd rather, first opt out."

Mike leaned back in his chair. "What are we doing tomorrow?"

"You know the show *Fear Factor?*" The guys nodded. "Something like that, only without the bugs. So if you want to avoid the slime, find your items first."

"And believe me, we have slime," Reilly said, laughing. "The scavenger hunt starts… now."

The men rose, their chairs protesting the movement with squeaks. Within seconds, the four men had divided themselves into two teams. They glanced over at Carter. "You coming?" Paul asked, but he didn't have much enthusiasm in his voice.

"Actually he's going to go it alone,"

Daphne said, surprising Carter as much as the design team. "I thought it might inspire you all a little more if you knew you had an opportunity to beat the boss."

The quick scramble out the door told Carter his employees had finally found the right incentive. "That was a good idea," he said to her after the men were gone. "Except for that golf project, things between me and my employees have been pretty strained."

"It'll get better," she said, laying a soft hand on his arm. "As the weekend goes on, you'll have more opportunities to work with the team and build a relationship with them."

"Sounds like a plan." Carter's interest right now *was* in building a relationship—but not with the men who worked for him. He took a step closer to Daphne, ostensibly reaching behind her for the paper he'd left on the table, but really only wanting to inhale her perfume. To be close to her again, after all those hours of separation, and then, of watching her while she talked, wanting everyone in the room to leave. "I'd rather work with you."

"I'm the coach. I'm not supposed to be

part of the…" Her words trailed off, caught in a breath as Carter moved closer and captured her face in his palms.

"I don't care about that right now. All I'm thinking about is you." His lips hovered over hers, a whisper away from a kiss. "I've wanted you since the minute I saw you in the airport. It's driven me crazy, being this close and not being able to touch you."

"It has?" she said, her voice soft and sweet, the scavenger hunt forgotten.

"Oh, yeah." He traced the outline of her lip with his thumb. Her jaw dropped open, and she tasted his finger, the tease nearly making Carter insane with a desire that had been steadily building ever since she'd stood outside his apartment with fire in her eyes.

"Daphne," he groaned, and in an instant, his mouth had met hers, this time with fire and heat, nothing simple, nothing sweet.

She responded in kind, wrapping her arms around him, drawing Carter closer, melding their bodies. Heat entwined them, desire whispering its siren song. Carter roamed his hands down the silky fabric of her shirt, over her waist, along the smooth curve of her buttocks. She moaned and arched her back, pressing against a part of him that was already in agony.

Carter had been with women before. He'd even thought he'd loved a few. But never had he felt this overwhelming need, this powerful want that seemed to echo throughout his senses. Every inch of him craved her with a need so powerful, he thought he'd go insane if he had to spend another moment away from her.

Was that desire? Or something more?

Something like…love?

"Daphne," he groaned against her lips, wanting nothing more than to take her upstairs, to quench his thirst. But even as he thought of doing that, he knew one night, one time in bed, would never be enough with Daphne Williams.

Her gaze met his, reflecting a mirror of his desire. A smile curved across her lips. "I think I can read your mind."

He leaned down and nuzzled her neck, eliciting a giggle from Daphne's throat. "How about a scavenger hunt…upstairs?"

"We shouldn't," she said, stretching her

chin upward, giving him better access, sighing as he trailed kisses along her throat and up to her mouth again, "but maybe…"

He bent over, scooping her into his arms. In seconds, Carter knew, he could have Daphne beneath him. He knew how it would begin, how it would end—

Especially how it would end.

He glanced down at her. Desire still coursed through his veins, but for the first time in his life, Carter wanted more than a one-night stand. Wanted more than to quench his physical appetite.

And ultimately, he knew, he'd be left feeling empty emotionally.

"What's wrong?" she asked when he stood there, her in his arms, but not one step closer to the bedroom.

"I want more." The words left him with the high pitch of surprise, of a man who had grown more in the last three days than he had in thirty-seven years.

"More?" Her brows knitted in confusion.

"I want to—" He drew in a breath. Carter Matthews had always led half a life. He'd never invested himself in anything more complex than eighteen holes on a par-three course. And where had it left him? Alone, unfulfilled, and…

Lost.

Until he'd met Daphne Williams and realized what he'd been searching for was already there, living two floors below him.

"You want what?" Daphne asked, her hand against his cheek, soft and warm. Filled with the kind of concern he'd never felt before.

His heart swelled, near to breaking, and in that moment, he knew.

He loved her.

As crazy as it sounded, as fast as it had happened, Carter Matthews had fallen in love with Daphne Williams. He didn't want to go home in a few days and go back to his apartment alone. He didn't want to wake up tomorrow without her by his side.

He didn't want to spend, in fact, one more day of his life alone.

But if he was smart, and did, for the first time in his life, what was better for her than what he wanted, he'd keep these feelings to himself. "I want to get out there and find that teddy bear." A grin crossed his face, but this one felt tight. "I can't let my guys beat me. I'll never live it down."

Then he walked away, knowing he was doing what was best. Even if it hurt like hell to do it.

Three hours later, the group sat on the floor of the expansive living room of the Boothbay Harbor house. The fireplace crackled, occasionally spitting a piece of ash onto the brick hearth. Daphne put a deck of cards into the center of the glass coffee table.

"What's that?" Paul asked.

"A game. It's like Truth or Dare, only without the running naked in the streets part."

"Bummer," Lenny muttered.

She laughed, then doled out the first set of cards. "Everyone take a look at their card, then ask the question on it of the person to your right. Paul, you go first."

Paul rolled his eyes, but did as she asked, turning to Lenny. "When you were ten, what did you think you were going to be when you grew up?"

"Easy. An *artiste*." Lenny laughed. "I was going to be the next Rembrandt."

"That explains why your drawings are always so detailed," Carter said. "You do have a knack for art."

"Thanks," Lenny said, a small but visible moment of connection. Then he picked up his card, and the game moved forward. "So, Carter," he said, reading off his card, "what's the craziest idea you ever had?"

"I asked Daphne to marry me."

Silence fell over the room, broken only by the crackle of burning logs.

"What'd she say?" Lenny asked. All eyes swiveled toward her.

"She turned me down," Carter said, also watching Daphne.

"Don't blame her," Paul muttered.

No one else said anything. Everyone waited, looking first to Carter, then to Daphne. "It, ah, wasn't good timing," she said.

"What about now?" Carter asked. "Is the timing better? Because I still want to marry you."

Reilly grinned like the Cheshire cat, but Daphne wasn't smiling.

"Carter—" She fidgeted with her cards, then rose. "We have a game to play. We can't discuss this right now."

"Fine," he said, then flipped over his card and turned to his right, toward her. "My card says—" and he flipped it toward her to prove it "...What is your heart's desire?"

She gave him a look like she suspected he'd dealt the card himself. "To be with someone who is honest. And true." Then she got to her feet. "I'm going for some more chips." She grabbed the already full bowl and left the room.

Reilly slipped into the place where she had been. "Well, let's continue. I'll take Daphne's turn."

Carter barely heard him. Instead he followed after Daphne. He pushed the swinging door and found her in the moonlit kitchen, yanking chips out of a plastic bag and dumping them into the bowl. "What did those chips ever do to you?"

She wheeled around. "Don't, Carter. Don't try and pretend that any of that was real."

He took a step closer, removing the chip bag from her hands before she did the

Ruffles any more damage. "It was real. I'm serious." The newfound feelings of love burst in his chest like a pyrotechnic display, the acknowledgment freeing the emotions. He peered down at her, and felt a smile curve across his face. Hell, across his whole body. "Daphne, I want to marry you. Tonight."

"Carter," she began, shaking her head. "We've been through this."

He took her hands in his. "This is different. I don't want to marry you to repair my reputation or to help you get funding or just because it's a whim, part of a game. I want to marry you because I've never met a woman who makes me feel like you do. I've fallen in—"

She put up a hand. "Don't say it, Carter. You can't feel anything for me yet. We've only just met. The whole thing is crazy."

"Yeah, it is." A foolish smile took over his face, filling him with an odd sense of excitement. "That's why we should do it."

"Just run off and get married?"

"Yeah." He thought of the sign he'd seen on the way over here, the advertisement on the chapel that had planted the seed of an idea. "We're in Boothbay Harbor. There's no waiting period. No blood tests. Nothing but you and me and a meeting with a justice of the peace."

She shook her head and pulled her hands out of his. "You're nuts. You seriously think we should let some guy in a suit with a little stamp determine the rest of our lives?" Daphne threw up her hands. "No, thank you. Besides, I hardly know you. Why don't you just go back to the game?"

He grinned, undaunted. "It'd be a great story to tell your grandkids someday."

For a second, Daphne thought she'd heard Carter say "our grandchildren." Then the rest of the word filtered in and she heard the "y," the implication that she would move on after Carter Matthews, marry someone else, maybe some guy with a name like John, who mowed the lawn twice a week, settled down with the paper and a coffee after dinner. They'd have kids, settle into a life of lasagna on Wednesdays and regular barbecues with the neighbors.

It sounded so dull. So…exactly what the usual Daphne would do, exactly what she had planned for herself ever since she was a little girl and watching her mother zip here and there, stability becoming a foreign word. Daphne had done that for years—followed the straight and narrow path, never stepped out of the box.

And where had it gotten her? Lonely, unhappy and as empty as the Grand Canyon.

"Marry me, Daphne." Carter's tempting grin tingled along her senses.

"But—"

"Do something spontaneous, Daphne. Something wild and unexpected."

"That's exactly what I try *never* to do."

"Which is exactly why you should do it," he said, taking her hands again in his, the grip confident and sure, feeling like a rock in a tumultuous ocean. "What's the worst that could happen?"

"We end up screaming at each other in divorce court?"

He ran a finger down the delicate slope of her nose. "Do you really think that'll happen to us?"

"It happens all the time."

"Yes, it does. To people who knew each

other for twenty years before they got married. And to people who ran off and eloped at the end of their first date."

She nodded. "Exactly."

"And then there are people who meet each other one day, fall in love in a heartbeat and stay married for fifty years. Life's a crapshoot, Daphne. Roll the dice."

"What if I roll a seven?"

"And what if you don't?"

She worried her bottom lip, trying to push away the temptation of the idea. The freedom inherent in a thought like eloping. "We could date, Carter. Like everyone else."

"I don't want to date. I don't want to take you to Chez Amore and then a little jazz club, and then, at the end of the night, bring you home and promise to call you in the morning. A promise I'll break, because I have never stuck to anything in my life." His gaze met hers, filled with the depth of honesty. "I'm tired of knowing the outcome before I even play the game. I don't want to live like that, Daphne. I don't want to feel empty anymore."

The echo of her own thoughts caught her

off guard, eroded her resolve. "What if you wake up tomorrow and realize you don't want to be stuck with me?"

He brushed back a tendril of her hair, the movement so gentle, so sweet, Daphne nearly cried. "I have dated a lot of women, but I have never come close to feeling for any of them what I feel for you right now."

Fear and a thousand what-ifs gripped her. "But—"

"Listen, what's the worst that can happen? You marry me, get your funding and in a few weeks, toss me to the curb?"

"And what do you get out of this?"

His smile was genuine. Strong. "You."

A whisper ran through her mind, carrying the thought that maybe he meant it. That maybe, as he'd said, he wanted her for more than restoring his reputation, saving his company. That he cared. Maybe even loved her. But that thought was too scary, too improbable, so she pushed it aside. "Carter, we should be smart about this."

"I'm done being smart, Daphne." He chuckled. "Maybe I never acted smart to begin with. All I know is that I want to marry you. I want to leap off that bridge and not worry about what's waiting below." He caught her hand, running his touch along her ring finger. "Do something unexpected, Daphne. Marry me."

"Something unexpected," she echoed, her gaze meeting his. Earnest truth shone in his eyes, and something within Daphne latched on to that, believing he was different. That this could work. "Yes, I'll marry you."

CHAPTER NINE

DAPHNE woke up in the morning with a different last name and a serious regret hangover.

What had she been thinking, marrying Carter Matthews?

She hadn't been thinking. He'd said the words "do something unexpected" and some rebellious streak appeared out of nowhere, voicing agreement. Before she knew it, they'd been in something called the Hideaway Chapel, standing before an Elvis impersonator with a Bible and a swivel in his hips.

Her cell phone rang. She groaned and reached for it, not feeling up to a call from anyone right now. "Hello?"

"Daph! There you are." Her mother's voice sounded tinny and far away. "I thought you'd call straight away after you got my letter."

Daphne pressed a hand to her eyes. "I've been busy. Working."

"Well, drop everything and come to London. Your mother needs you."

Daphne sighed. "I can't. I have a company to run. Clients who count on me."

"Don't be so dull, Daphne. You can always find a job here. I need you to help me with all this doctor gobbledy-gook."

Daphne thought of the hundreds of times she had done as her mother asked. Changing schools, neighborhoods, shifting one life for another because her mother had wanted to move. "Mother, I—"

"Now don't say no. Not yet. Think about it."

Daphne raised her hand off her temples. The gold ring Carter had slipped on her finger last night caught a glint of sunlight and shone like a beacon. "I can't," Daphne said, her resolve cementing as the words left her mouth.

"You...what? I think our connection is scratchy because I thought you said you can't."

"I did say that. I can't up and leave here. I'm building that creativity center—"

"Oh, that again."

Daphne gritted her teeth before she said something she'd regret. "It's important to me. You'll have to find someone else to help you. A social worker or nurse or something."

"I thought I could count on you," Mary said, her tone now annoyed.

"And I'd thought the same about you." But the words were spoken into an empty phone. Her mother had hung up before Daphne could respond.

Daphne stared at the cell for a long time. She'd vowed never to become her mother, and here she was, repeating the very same mistakes.

A knock sounded on her door. Daphne scrambled out of bed, grabbed her robe and stuffed her arms into the sleeves. She drew in a deep breath before opening the door.

Carter.

"Good morning, Mrs. Matthews," he said, a grin on his face.

The last two words slammed into her. She really had done it—stood there and said her

"I do's" while an elderly woman with pink plastic curlers on her head played a piano accompaniment. "Good morning," Daphne replied, because she couldn't think of another thing to say that didn't begin with "Did we really…" or end with "bad idea."

"I brought you coffee." He held up a steaming mug.

"Oh, you are the best." She took the cup from him, inhaled the scent of the brew, then took a sip. The perfect blend of cream and sugar greeted her taste buds. "How did you know how I took my coffee?"

"Reilly. He, ah, noticed my ring this morning."

Daphne groaned. Once Reilly was hooked on that, there'd be no stopping him. He'd crow about what a good idea it had been, when Daphne knew marrying Carter had been the exact opposite. "Did he tell anyone?"

Carter shook his head. "But he did call someone named Elton. I overheard him say they needed to plan a proper reception for us."

"Oh Lord." What had she done? And even more—how was she going to undo this mistake before it got worse? "I think I need to add some rum to this."

Carter laughed. "Exactly the thought I had this morning." He took a step forward, leaning against the oak jamb of the door. "But then I thought about it, and realized it's not so bad being married. Especially to you."

She arched a brow. "Not so bad? As opposed to a step above being put on the rack and tortured?"

He chuckled again. The sound of the shower being turned on echoed in the hall, the old pipes banging a protest. Undoubtedly, one of Carter's employees. "May I come in?"

"Sure," she said, feeling odd about inviting him in and equally odd about the fact that he was her husband now and had every right to be in her bedroom.

Carter took a step closer, teasing at her hair with a finger, while he shut the door behind him. Leaving them alone. And with a whole lot of unfinished business from last night brewing between them. They'd returned to the house after the ceremony, enjoying some steamy kisses in the car and the hall before one of the designers came down for a midnight snack.

And woke Daphne out of the fog wrapped around her ever since Carter had proposed. She'd snuck off to her bedroom—alone— already realizing she'd done the worst thing she could have—

Turned into her mother.

How many times had she vowed she'd never turn her own life upside down like that?

"You look beautiful," he said softly.

"No, I don't." A nervous, self-conscious tremor sounded in her voice. "I'm rumpled and sleep deprived and—"

"Beautiful." The grin curved across his face again. "And don't forget, also my wife."

"Carter—"

He put a finger to her mouth. "Don't. I can see the argument already on your lips. Let's go about our day, and get used to this idea."

"The idea that we possibly made a huge mistake last night?"

"Or the best decision we ever made." He gave her one quick kiss, then left the room.

Daphne stood there until her legs stiffened with disuse, weighed down with regret. And wishing she could rewind her life.

After a hearty breakfast cooked by Reilly, Daphne gathered the men around the ping-pong table. In the shower that morning, she'd vowed to concentrate on work, not Carter. She'd shove the marriage certificate—and its ramifications—into her suitcase and pray the old out-of-sight, out-of-mind adage worked.

In the corner, Reilly sent her the occasional smirk, which she answered with a don't-you-dare-tell-anyone glare. Daphne picked up two ping-pong paddles and handed them to Lenny and Mike. "This is more than a normal ping-pong game. With each hit, you have to tell your opponent something about yourself."

Paul's face scrunched up. "Tell me this isn't some touchy-feely Dr. Phil thing where we all sit around singing 'Kumbaya' and roasting marshmallows."

Daphne laughed. "No, not at all. It's just an exercise designed to help you get to know each other better. You can say anything you like, something personal, or career related. The point is to continue the team building we've already begun."

"You don't think we did enough of that out there while we were looking for the frying pans in the trees?" Mike asked, sending a glance Reilly's way.

Reilly shrugged, a tease on his face. "Good thing you found it or we would have been having carrot sticks for breakfast."

The guys groaned, but Daphne could tell they had enjoyed the time with Reilly and the fact that they'd beat Carter by a mile. They hadn't even noticed, in fact, that she and Carter had been gone for a few hours that night. They'd been too busy rehashing the game with Reilly, staying up late with lots of laughs and a few beers, igniting a slew of ideas that they scribbled across scratch pads Daphne had provided.

"Every exercise we've done has been to build on the one before. The theory is if you're working together as a team, you're thinking as a team. I can tell, judging by the ideas you came up with last night, that this is working."

"And how does this—" Lenny held up a green paddle "—help our creativity?"

"It doesn't. Exactly."

Paul threw up his hands. "Then why are we wasting our time? Shouldn't we spend more time sketching ideas for the fall lineup instead of playing more? I thought you were supposed to be some creative expert."

She'd thought so, too, until she got a little too creative with her personal life. She avoided Carter's gaze and refocused on the two men beside the ping-pong table. "When you're working together as a team, you create an environment where creativity can thrive and grow. I believe all of you already have those talents inside you, or you wouldn't be in the jobs you are. The key is to find a way to open that up again, to get you to expand your horizons and your thinking, more than you already have."

Mike shrugged. "Still sounds like some psychobabble to me, but I'll try it."

"Great." Daphne put Lenny at one end of the table, Mike at the other. At first, as the ping-pong ball made its journey back and forth, the men didn't share anything more meaningful than the fact that they shared a liking for pork and beans. Then, as the match wore on, they began to open up.

"I'm an only child," Mike said.

"And I come from a family of six," Lenny replied, smacking the white ball. It bounced off the table with a hollow ping.

"I live at home with my mother," Mike added, then blushed. "Uh, just while I'm searching for an apartment."

Lenny snickered, which made him miss the ball—and lose the match. They worked through the rest of the design team, with Lenny finally losing to Paul in the final round. "Now you get to play Carter," Daphne said to Paul. The designer shot Carter a grin.

Daphne shooed Carter into place and put a paddle in his hand. "It'll be good for you and good for the company," she whispered. "I promise."

"You ready?" Paul said to him. "Because this game isn't for wimps."

Daphne saw Carter bristle at the comment, but he bit back a retort and readied his swing. "Go right ahead."

"I'm thirty-four," Paul said, then hit the ball over the tiny net.

"Thirty-seven here," Carter replied, hitting it back.

"I've been designing toys for fifteen years," Paul said, waiting for the ball to bounce before he connected with it again. "How about you?"

Daphne again saw Carter bite back a flare of temper at the clear disregard from his employee. If Carter was ever going to build a team with these men, he'd have to open up and show them he was a man who deserved their respect—and not just because of his title. "I'd never played much with toys when I was a kid."

"That explains a lot," Paul said with a snort.

"Share a fact, not an opinion," Daphne cautioned.

"I have a twin brother," Carter said.

"And I could run this company," Paul said, skipping the pleasantries and getting very honest very fast. "Better than you."

Tension crackled in the room. The other three designers fell silent, waiting for

Carter's reaction. The ball bounced onto his side of the table and he bunted it back. "A hundred times in the last few weeks, I could have fired you," he said, "but I haven't. Do you know why?"

The comment surprised Paul. He forgot to swing and the little white ball bounced off the edge of the green table. "Why?"

Carter laid his paddle down. "Because, SuperClean Man aside, you are a damned good designer. If your attitude would match your talent, we might actually get somewhere."

Paul scoffed. "Like you care. You're just in this for the money."

"I don't draw a paycheck," Carter said. "I haven't taken a dime from this company since I inherited it."

Lenny, Mike, Paul and Jason gaped at him. "No paycheck? Really?"

"I took this job not because Uncle Harry gave it to me or because I missed out on my childhood but because I had something to prove," he continued. "I thought I could be more than the guy who golfs and drives a fast car." Carter skirted the table and came up to Paul. "But I haven't done that, have I?"

Paul shook his head, mute.

"Doesn't matter anymore," Carter said. He glanced around the room, taking in the men who had been his employees for the last few months. They'd never worked with him, only against him. Uncle Harry's spotty leadership and then prolonged absence had clearly created a climate that encouraged the men to take the reins. Or, maybe, like his father, they saw only the Gloria's Gossip and Gab version of Carter. "I don't have to prove anything. Not anymore."

"Because you're going to quit," Paul said, as if he already knew the answer.

Emotions flickered over Carter's face. Daphne held her breath, sure he was going to do just as Paul predicted. The Carter Matthews she had read about in the paper would have gotten mad and quit. He'd have walked away, moving on to the next thing without a second thought.

But the Carter Matthews she had married last night…

She suspected he'd do the very opposite.

"I'm not quitting," Carter said, and a tiny cheer sounded in Daphne's head. "Instead

I'm putting some new incentives in place. This afternoon, Daphne told me you have a brainstorming session. I'm sure you'll come up with plenty of great ideas. And for that, I'd like to offer a prize."

That got the men's attention. "What kind of prize?"

"The first man to come up with a bona-fide hit of a toy gets—"

The men were silent, watching Carter. "My car," he said.

"Your car?" Mike's voice rose with surprise. "But you love that Lexus. It's a total babe-magnet."

Carter's gaze swiveled to Daphne's. "Exactly why I don't need it anymore."

Then he walked away, leaving a stunned group behind.

Daphne found Carter later, standing on the wraparound porch, holding a bottle of beer. The men had gone into town with Reilly for dinner, which she knew was part of a ploy by Reilly to allow her and Carter time alone.

Something Daphne wasn't sure she needed. She couldn't trust the riot of emotions running through her every time she looked at Carter. And, she apparently couldn't trust her better judgment, either, whenever he was around.

"What was that about earlier?"

"An incentive." He took a long pull off the bottle of beer, then placed it on the railing. "And after this, I'm going to find a competent CEO who can run this company the way it should be."

"Are you taking the easy way out?"

He wheeled around. "You think this is easy? I took over that company, convinced this was my shot to show I could do something with my life. If anything, all I've done is make it worse."

"Companies fail, Carter, and it's not always the CEO's fault."

"Yeah, but I'm the one where the buck stops. And the bucks definitely stopped after I took over. I think it's best for all involved if I do what I always do."

"Quit," she said, finishing the sentence.

He shrugged. "I dropped out of college. Never stayed with a job for more than a few months. Never married—"

"Until last night," Daphne said.

"Yeah." His gaze met hers.

"Well, don't worry about that," she replied, a surprising hurt stinging in her chest that he, too, saw it as a mistake, "we'll find a way to undo that as soon as we get home."

"What if I don't want to?"

"Carter, be a realist. It'll never work. We were clearly not thinking last night." She drew in a breath and faced reality. "You're going to wake up one morning. Maybe not tomorrow, maybe not next month, but you will wake up one morning and realize that eloping with me was a huge mistake."

"What makes you think that?" he asked, his gaze still on hers, so intent, so serious.

"Because I lived it, Carter. I had a mother who made marrying a sport. Who thought nothing of just up and taking off to Bermuda for the weekend. Or enrolling in a belly dancing class because she saw it in some movie. Or forgetting to fill the fridge because she was too busy taking up tai chi or yoga or something. I will not be that woman, regardless of what happened last night."

"And you think this meant nothing to me, that I did it because I had a half a beer in me and nothing better to do?"

Put that way, it sounded harsh and mean, but Daphne knew, as surely as she knew her own name, that regret was a huge chaser to spontaneity. "Yeah."

He took a step back, grabbing up his drink again. A shadow draped its darkness over him. A long moment passed, punctuated only by the call of a night bird and the distant sound of a plane. "I suppose you're right."

Hurt shaded his voice, but Daphne ignored it. Ending it with him was the best thing for both of them, before either of them got too wrapped up in thinking these feelings were real. "Don't quit your job," she said, returning to the safe ground of work talk. "You can do this."

He snorted. "Even my assistant says that, as she hands me another profit and loss made up of negative numbers."

Daphne moved into the shadow with him. Moonlight played across his features, like Nature's strobe light. "You're so much more than you think you are, Carter. I've seen it in the way you interacted with those guys today. In the way you talk about the business. You have everything a CEO needs. If you'd just adjust that attitude to go with your talent, we might have something here."

"Using my own words against me?"

"They were good ones." She took the beer from his hand and laid it on the railing, then clasped both his hands with hers. "You have good instincts. You know what to do, where to cut, how to make the most of every deal. Look at how you networked on the golf course, talked up my creativity center with your clients. You're just not using those talents at work."

"So you're saying I should play more golf?"

She laughed. "No. But you should take that famous Matthews charm and use it in your business dealings."

"Do what I do best and schmooze?"

She nodded. "Pearl seems to have the financial end under control. That leaves you free to do the rest. Sell your products, Carter, as well as you sold yourself to me."

He reached up and cupped her chin, his

thumb tracing an enticing trail along her jaw. "But I never sealed the deal, did I? And I didn't do a very good job of selling if you're divorcing me without ever consummating the marriage."

"I..." She shook her head, the words in her head flitting away into the night air.

"Don't you want me, Daphne?"

How easy it would be to lie. To turn away and pretend she hadn't enjoyed any of those kisses. Hadn't thought a thousand times over about going to bed with Carter.

"Yes, I do," she said, the words a breath that caught in her throat.

"Good. At least we agree on one thing." He lowered his head, brought his mouth to hers and drifted a soft kiss across her lips.

Unbidden, her arms stole around his waist, pulling him closer. In the darkness, every touch, every breath, intensified. Want curled a tight grip around Daphne, holding her there, making every reservation she'd had disappear into the night. Carter's touch was magic, awakening nerve endings too long held dormant, restrained by Daphne's fear of making a mistake.

He slipped a hand between them, cupping the soft flesh of her breast, igniting an explosion inside of Daphne more powerful than she had felt with anyone. Ever. It frightened and excited her, as if being with Carter was an amusement park ride, sending her emotions careening up hills and over curves, lifting her off the edge of her seat, and yanking her back again.

He pulled his mouth away from hers, lowering his head to trail tender, hot kisses along her throat, murmuring her name. Desire washed over, then was followed by an emotion so strong, so powerful, it bordered on a riptide.

She was falling for Carter Matthews. Getting swept up into the fantasy. The belief that this could be real.

Daphne jerked away from him. "We can't do this, Carter. I need to be practical. Smart. And being with you is as far from that as I can get."

"Daphne—"

"No, Carter. I won't make decisions because I believe there's something between us when there really isn't. I want the whole enchilada. I want love and a house and a

CHAPTER TEN

THE return trip marked a change for Carter. He had no doubt the business could do well now, particularly with a slew of new toy ideas that were sure to be hits. His designers, who had avoided him on the flight out, now opted to cluster around him, chatting excitedly about the future. They had ideas and wanted to share them—

With him.

He couldn't have been more surprised if Cemetery Kitty had come back to life.

After he'd issued that challenge, the men had gotten to work, finally seeking him out and including him in the brainstorming. They'd vied for his attention at first, wanting him to judge the best idea.

They'd ended up grouped around the fireplace, with popcorn and endless supplies of blank paper and pencils. Daphne and Reilly had slipped into the background, leaving the five of them to do exactly what she'd predicted—

Bond.

Then, as they'd talked and he'd encouraged this idea, tweaked that one, gotten excited about the recorder that let preschoolers create a mini-CD, the dynamics had shifted.

And so had something in Carter.

He began to feel as if he belonged. As if he had finally found the right shaped-hole for his human peg. The dual feelings of inclusion and success were so foreign, it took a while before they sank in and resonated.

He'd managed to make a change in every area of his life. Except for his personal life. That had backfired like a badly tuned car, exploding in his face and erasing every bit of ground he'd thought he'd made with Daphne in the last few days.

Somehow, he needed to find a way to rectify that. To get her to talk to him about something other than work. Because the feelings that had inspired him to run off and elope had done nothing but grow over this weekend.

Apparently a weekend away at a cozy Maine retreat was good for a lot more than recharging the brain's creativity cells.

Daphne's quiet touch, her teasing smile, her quirky glasses—all of it gave his day an edge he'd never had before. Something to look forward to—

A future. Maybe even a house with a fence, kids. A dog—a much smaller dog than Grover, but a dog all the same. It was what she had said she wanted, and in some ironic twist that had turned Carter the playboy into Carter the married man, so now did he.

"Thank you," he said, taking her hand. She had sat beside him—thank God for assigned seating and a nearly full plane—but ignored him by working on a planner pad since takeoff.

She smiled that smile he had grown to know as well as his own face. "Just doing my job."

"You did more than that. I know this is going to sound corny, but you changed my life."

She put down her pen and took her glasses off her nose, dangling them from one finger.

"No, you did that yourself. You had everything you needed already inside you, Carter. All you needed was a push in the right direction."

Daphne believed in him. And that confidence hit him as hard as a sledgehammer. "A shove was more like it." He studied their clasped palms. "What's going to happen when we get home?"

"I'll get to work on the final details for the creativity center, you'll be busy putting those new designs into production—"

"I meant with us."

"I don't know," she said, her gaze darting away from his, leaving her as unreadable as a stone.

"I suppose it all depends," Carter replied.

"On what?"

"On whether you want to live on the second floor or the fourth."

A long, heavy sigh escaped her. "Carter, what happened that night was one of those spur-of-the-moment mistakes. Let's just forget the whole thing."

Disappointment slammed into him. Everything had gone so well in the last few days, and he'd begun to think that maybe that rainbow of success would extend between him and Daphne, too. "I don't want this to end, Daphne," he said, trying, but failing, to catch her eye. "I'm in love with you."

She shook her head, and the disappointment quadrupled in weight. "We hardly know each other."

"That's what the next fifty years are for." He gave her a grin, but she didn't echo the gesture. He was losing ground here, fast, and had no idea how to stop it.

"I won't do this, Carter. I won't make the mistakes my mother did." She drew her hand out of his and clasped her two together, preventing him from holding her again. "I'm getting an annulment as soon as we get back to Indiana. I'm sorry." She rose from her seat and moved to one several rows back.

For the first time in his life, Carter Matthews had everything he wanted—except the woman he loved. Carter pulled his cell phone out of his pocket and held it tightly. As soon as this plane landed, he'd give Daphne what she wanted.

And pray it would be enough.

* * *

Daphne unpacked her clothes, threw a load of laundry into the basement washer and straightened her apartment, but all the activity did nothing to quiet the storm inside her. She glanced up at the ceiling twice, three times, thinking of Carter, two floors up. Her husband—

At least for now. In the morning, she intended to change that. It was the only sensible thing to do.

Her doorbell rang and she jumped to open it, half expecting Carter there, to plead his case again, as he had in the airport, outside at the taxi stand, and on her cell phone, but every time, she had shut him off and told him her mind was made up.

"Mother!" Daphne said.

"Hullo, Daphne," her mother said, breezing in, and depositing two giant suitcases by the door. She drew her daughter into a quick embrace that smelled of Chanel No. 5.

"Where's Brad? Don't tell me you left him in the hospital." If her mother was on her doorstep, it meant one thing—she was escaping and looking for Daphne to support her newest adventure.

Mary drew back and waved a dismissive hand. "He didn't need me. He has all those nurses. Let's not talk of hospitals and illness," Mary said, her voice taking on a British accent, as if she'd been in London for years instead of months. "Let's talk of happy things, shall we?"

Daphne sighed and moved back, gesturing her mother toward the living room, but Mary diverted to the kitchen. "How about a spot of tea?" Mary said.

"You don't drink tea."

Her mother grinned. "Then let's just have the brandy I was going to put in it anyway."

Daphne fixed her mother a drink, declined to join in on the festivities and instead took up the opposite seat at the kitchen table.

Her mother cupped her hand around the snifter, took a long gulp, then set it back on the table. "I'm divorcing Brad."

"Now? The man is in the *hospital*. And he loves you."

That Daphne knew well, having seen her mother and Brad together several times. He had an undying devotion to her, and had always put up with all her quirks and crazy ideas.

Her mother shook her head. "I'm not like you. I can't stay in one place. I can't be *dependable*." She shuddered.

"No, Mother, you're wrong," Daphne said, meeting her mother's gaze with direct honesty. "You *weren't* dependable. Past tense. But you can be. All you have to do is choose. Brad deserves a woman who will stick it out through thick and thin." The anger bubbled over into Daphne's words. "Just as he did with you."

Mary drew back, her hands leaving the snifter to worry together in her lap. "That was different."

"No, it wasn't. Mother, when you had that breast cancer scare, he was *there*. He held your hand, he sat through every doctor's visit. He brought you breakfast in bed *every day*, for Pete's sake." Even Daphne, who had stayed at her mother's house for two weeks that summer, hadn't dispensed that much TLC.

"I know, and I feel terrible."

Daphne rose, biting back the anger that had exploded in her chest. "No, you don't.

You always think about you and no one else. When I was a kid, you always ran off, leaving me to my own devices. And then, whenever I tried to do something fun, like get into that art school, you shot it down, as if I was about to go on a murder spree. You made me be the responsible, dependable one when it should have been you."

"I only wanted to protect you," Mary said.

"From what? Overuse of pastels? I just wanted to spread my wings. Try something new."

"I wanted to protect you," Mary said, her hands again going to the snifter, her finger tracing the rim before she met her daughter's eyes. "From turning out like me."

Daphne sunk back into her chair, speechless. Never had she imagined that was the reason her mother had held her back.

"That's exactly what I did," Daphne said softly, seeing the pieces put together now. "I didn't take any chances. I didn't live by the seat of my pants." Until she'd married Carter Matthews.

"Are you kidding me?" Mary said. "You own a business. Tell me that's not jumping off a cliff every day and hoping there's some water to break your fall."

"Well, in work, yes, but not in my personal life."

"Do you want to know why I married all those men?" her mother asked. "Why I couldn't stay in one place for very long?" Her mother paused, then went on. "Because after your father died, no one could ever take his place. And I couldn't stay where all those memories were. It was killing me, Daphne, bit by bit." She took a sip of the brandy, then clutched the glass like a lifeline. "I was a mess after your father died and the best thing I could have done was leave you."

"No, Mother," Daphne said softly. "The best thing you could have done was to be there for me. You were the only mother I had." She sucked in a breath, wishing she held the brandy now as the truth began to rise up inside her, overriding the hurts and disappointments, replacing it with the honesty of age, of experience. "You were the only mother I wanted. I didn't need you to be perfect. I just needed you to be there."

Mary lifted her gaze to her daughter's,

tears shimmering in eyes so like Daphne's they could have been twins. "You *wanted* me around?"

"Of course I did. I just didn't know how to tell you."

Mary toyed with the glass, her shoulders tense and tight, and for a second, Daphne thought she would bolt, as she always had whenever anything serious was discussed. "Do you still want me around?"

Daphne looked at the woman who had given birth to her, raised her and abandoned her, sometimes at the same time. And who had never encouraged her daughter's dreams, out of some crazy thought that she was protecting Daphne.

And yet, how much of that had been her mother's fault—and how much was Daphne's own for not speaking up as she got older, for retreating into the safety of schedules and stability so that she, too, could avoid the chaos that her father's death had launched?

For letting thirty-five years go by before she had the conversation they both needed?

Daphne thought of Carter, of how he'd

finally taken a chance, leaping into unknown territory even though he'd risked rejection and failure. Perhaps the coach needed to take a few lessons from the client.

"Yeah," Daphne said, reaching for her mother's hand, vowing a new start for both of them, a merging of their worlds, "I do. Let's start over, Mother. A blank page, right here." Wasn't that how she approached her business? What she taught her clients? When something wasn't working, throw it aside and try a whole new line of thinking on a brand-new sheet of paper. "But for now, you should go back to take care of Brad. And I'll come out to London this summer and visit you."

"You will?" Her mother's voice held the vulnerability of a child's. How odd that the roles had been reversed, with Daphne the one now dispensing the hope.

"Yes, I will."

Her mother's grip tightened, building a thread that had gone unraveled for too many years. "Okay, I'll try. Staying put terrifies me, Daph."

"And running off on a tangent terrifies

me. Maybe we can have the best of each other's worlds."

Her mother nodded. "I'd like that."

They sat there and talked until the wee hours of the morning, making up for lost ground. Eventually Daphne told her mother about her marriage to Carter, and found a kindred understanding in Mary's eyes and words.

As Mary headed off to bed, an envelope caught under the door snagged Daphne's attention. Her name was scrawled across the front in red crayon.

Inside was a check, made out to the creativity center for the remainder of the funding she needed. Signed by Carter, from his own personal account. On the memo line, he'd written, "Believe in the impossible, Daphne. Sometimes it comes true."

She slipped the check into the front pocket of her bag. As she did, her fingers brushed a small, hard piece of plastic.

The lone army man. She held it for a long time, then decided a little outflanking was in order.

CHAPTER ELEVEN

MONDAY morning brought Carter a renewed enthusiasm for his job. The retreat had definitely turned the tide at TweedleDee Toys. If he could resurrect this company, he could do about anything.

Which hopefully meant he could also get through to Daphne and salvage what he had clearly ruined with that crazy idea of eloping.

He'd left the check under her door last night, sure he'd hear from her this morning. But she hadn't called. Hadn't stopped by. Hadn't answered her phone this morning.

Clearly he was going to have to get a little creative if he was going to find a way to get close to her again.

Pearl met him in the parking lot, waving a sheaf of papers. "You'll never believe it, Mr. Matthews. We have *orders*."

"Already?" he asked, as the two of them strode into the building and toward his office.

"Those sketches from the retreat that you faxed over to Toy Castle last night were a huge hit. They placed a *half a million* dollar order." Pearl's eyes widened and Carter could swear he saw her nearly tear up. "They want that Ninja girl doll to be *the* rollout toy for the holiday season. Apparently a girl who can kick a little butt is needed in the toy marketplace." A smile curved across Pearl's face. "You did it," she said. "You turned it around."

"It wasn't just me," Carter said, reaching the design team room, where the four men were indulging in celebratory doughnuts and coffee. "This was a team effort."

Paul looked up from his chocolate glazed and gave Carter a thumbs-up. "When you have a minute, Mr. Matthews, I have a couple sketches I worked out last night. I had a brainstorm after I got home and saw my kids. I'm thinking cats—" he put up a hand to ward off Carter's groan "—that have some life. Combine the care and feeding aspects of those Tamagotchi pocket toys with a stuffed animal."

Carter smiled. "That's a great idea. Takes

interactive to a whole new level. And, it's not dead. My favorite kind of toy." He gestured toward the furry body of Cemetery Kitty, resting peacefully above a white paper cross taped to the file cabinet. Then he reached in his pocket, pulled out his car keys and dropped them into Paul's palm.

"Mine?" Paul said, surprised.

Carter nodded. "You earned it." He congratulated the guys, then headed to his office. He'd called his father earlier this morning and asked him to come by for a meeting. Kelly's nod told Carter that his father had arrived.

Carter greeted Jonathon, then waved him into the office and shut the door. "What's this about?" Jonathon asked. "I have to be in court in an hour."

Carter took a seat behind his desk and waited until his father had done the same. "I have some news that I wanted to tell you in person. Before Gloria gets a hold of it and blasts it all over her column." Carter drew in a breath. "I got married this weekend. To Daphne Williams."

His father's eyes widened in shock.

"Married? To the woman with the creativity thing?"

Carter nodded. "She's also the one responsible for my newly charged design team." He grinned. "And a whole lot more."

The shock abated, replaced by a scowl. "Do you love this woman or was it another of your spur-of-the-moment decisions?" His father let out a long breath. "When I told you to settle down, I never thought you'd actually do it. Don't tell me you got married to spite me."

"I love her." Carter had no doubts about that—though whether Daphne felt the same, he didn't know. Either way, he was determined not to let her go. To find a way to win her heart.

Forever.

His father shook his head and let out a little snort. "You'll find out soon enough that it won't last. Just do me a favor and keep the ending out of the paper."

Carter exploded out of his seat. "Why can't you be happy for me? Why do you tear apart everything I do?"

"Because you make bad decisions."

"No. I make decisions you don't agree

with. That doesn't make them bad." And then, Carter knew. The pieces fell into place, one after another. His father's derision of marriage, of commitment to a woman. All those years of bitterness, built up from one spring day and one woman's choice. "Mom walked out on you, Dad, and she was wrong for doing that. But that doesn't mean you have to tear down any possibility for happiness that I, or Cade—or hell, even you— might have."

"I don't do that."

"Bull. All you do is rip us apart. Especially me, because I wasn't as smart as Cade. I didn't go to college and work for the family firm. But now I've got a job, I'm running a company. I'm married. And I'm happy, damn it."

Carter drew in a breath, facing his father square-on, no longer couching his words, worrying that he might once again disappoint. "Why can't you finally say, 'Good job, Carter? I'm proud of you, son'?" Shards of hurt ran through his words, sharpening the edges until they seemed to slice him as quickly as they did the air between them. "Why was I never good enough for you?"

His father's gaze locked on Carter's for a long, hot second, and then he tore it away and sank farther into his chair. He seemed to curl into himself, his spine losing some of its starch, his face aging. "Because *I* wasn't good enough," he said, the words nearly a whisper.

Carter dropped into the opposite chair, studying the carpet at his shoes, knowing that if he looked at his father now, the moment would disappear in the bravado of masculinity. "You ran that law firm single-handedly for years. You raised Cade and I. What on earth do you think you weren't good enough for?"

"She left me, Carter. Walked right on out and left me."

The memory came back in slivered images. Army men. Sandbox hills. Dark brown suitcase. Short, sensible heels. And a quick, see-you-in-a-minute kiss that had turned into never-see-you-again. Carter sucked in a breath, holding all of those memories there, keeping them tight inside his chest, refusing to let them do their damage again. "She left us all, Dad. I wasn't good enough, either."

"It was never you. Or Cade. She left *me,*

Carter. I was the one who screwed up." He drew in a breath. "I cheated on her. And I broke her heart."

Carter's gaze leapt to his father's. "You did?" Upstanding model citizen Jonathon Matthews had had an affair?

"It was over as fast as it began, but your mother found out and left. If I hadn't done that, maybe…" His father didn't finish.

Carter shook his head. "*She* left her kids behind, Dad. Not just you. She never looked back. Never contacted us again. She could have divorced you, Dad. Shared custody. Seen her boys."

"Yeah, she could have," Jonathon admitted.

The question of why rose in Carter, but he didn't voice it. The answer no longer mattered. His mother had been the one who lost out, not Carter and Cade. He was thirty-seven now. Far past the age where he needed milk and cookies at the end of the day. He had his father. He had Cade.

And now, he had Daphne. Vanessa Matthews had been the real loser in this equation.

"After your mother left," his father went on, also studying his shoes, apparently from the same school of macho as his son, "I was overwhelmed. Two small boys, a business, a thousand cases on my desk."

"So you became a perfectionist," Carter said, seeing his neat office and knowing he shared more than one trait with his father.

"It was my way of keeping order. Of making sure none of us screwed up again. Especially me." His father raised his gaze now and met his son's. "I didn't want either of you to walk out, too."

"Dad, we were five. We were afraid to walk to the corner without an adult."

Jonathon chuckled a little, the moment of levity allowing each of them to find a little distance from the emotions crackling in the air; feelings neither had surrendered before. "Yeah, I know. But I still couldn't afford a mistake. It became my way of coping, or whatever the psychologists would say. I guess I started expecting the same of you two."

"I was no picnic to raise, either," Carter said, thinking of all the mud—and trouble—he'd gotten into as a child, then as an adult, but only in a more public manner.

Jonathon's eyes softened with memories.

"Yeah, you were the challenging one. Always determined to blaze your own path."

Carter looked around his office. "And I finally made that work." He told his father about Daphne, the retreat and the result. When he was done, his father wore the one thing Carter had never expected to see.

A smile.

"The guys really pulled it together," Carter said. "The design team—"

"No, Carter, *you* did this," his father cut in. "A company needs a leader in order to move forward." He paused, out of his element in this moment of sharing, of compliments. "I'm proud of you, son. Damned proud."

Carter could have taken his father to task for all those years of disparaging comments. Instead he said simply, "Thanks, Dad."

His father nodded and cleared his throat. "It's long overdue."

"Hey! You can't go in there!" Outside the closed door, Kelly's high-pitched voice reached mega decibels of panic. "He's in a meeting!"

"I can go anywhere I damned well please. Besides, that's my clown in there."

Carter and Jonathon both popped out of

their seats and turned to look at each other. The door burst open and in walked a ghost.

"Well, howdy-ho, all. Nothing like a little return from the dead to start your Monday off right."

"Uncle Harry?" Carter's jaw dropped open and he had to blink twice before he was sure he wasn't hallucinating.

"In the flesh," his uncle said, patting at his ample barrel-shaped chest, very much alive and well. He still had the same full head of white hair, the unibrow that danced with his laughter and the rainbow suspenders that were his trademark. "So, how'd you guys like my little joke? I love it when I pull one over on someone and this one, I gotta say, was a doozy."

"Joke?" Jonathon asked, the same look of shock on his face. "You were declared legally dead."

Uncle Harry chuckled, as if the whole thing was one big late-night monologue. "I should have been declared legally capable of a hell of a disappearing act. I bet Harry Houdini is watching me, jealous as all heck that he didn't think of this."

"You *planned* this?" Carter said.

"Yep." Harry grinned, clearly pleased with himself. "Wanted to see how our little Carter here would do wearing my shoes." Harry looked down at his feet. "Whoops. I'm a size twelve. I bet they didn't fit very well."

"You did this because you thought I'd make a good family joke?" Carter asked.

Uncle Harry laughed and waved a hand of dismissal. "You were the only one I could have pulled a prank like this on. Lord knows my brother is nothing but a huge stick in the tar pits." He cast a disgusted look Jonathon's way. "I couldn't have put him in charge of a *toy* company, for Pete's sake. He'd be selling organizers to two-year-olds."

"That's because I'm practical," Jonathon said. "I don't treat life like a giant joke."

"Dull, dull, dull," Uncle Harry said, sending his eyes heavenward.

"Responsible," Carter cut in. "My father didn't tear off on crazy ideas because he had a family to raise. He didn't have the same luxuries as you did. You were a bachelor. You had no one but yourself to think of."

"Thank you, Carter," Jonathon said softly.

Carter turned toward the man who had been more adversary than parent for so long and gave him a smile. They'd built a bridge in the last few minutes and Carter intended to keep on adding sticks in the weeks, months and years to come. "I get it now, Dad. You did the best you could."

"No, not the best," his father replied, his voice gruff. "I could have done better by both of you."

"And who do you think I remind you of? You and all your talk about responsibility," Uncle Harry said to Carter. "Why do you think I gave you the company in the first place?"

"To teach me a lesson?"

"No, to get you to grow up a little. Something I never did. And now you have, so," Uncle Harry said, dusting his hands together, "while I'd love to continue this touching family moment, I have a company to run. Carter, thanks for baby-sitting. You're free to leave and go back to the golf course."

"No."

The three men wheeled around at the single word, spoken in concert. The design team stood in the doorway, a beaming Pearl behind them, and Kelly beside them, clearly the messenger. "We don't want Carter to leave," Paul said.

Uncle Harry chuckled. "Ah, pulling a fast one on the prankster, are ya? Get back to work guys. I'll hold a meeting in a minute. Whoopee cushions all around the conference room."

"We're serious," Paul said. "If you take over again, we're quitting. When you ran this company, you had plenty of jokes but no input. You're terrible with finances, worse with employees."

"Hey, I resemble that remark," Uncle Harry said.

"Then you might want to embark on that improv career you kept talking about," Mike said. "Because we want Carter in charge here."

"A mutiny, aye?" Harry looked from one man to the other, the smile slowly disappearing from his face. "Well, if that's how you feel about it…"

"We do."

Harry stood there a long time, his face as sober as a judge's. Then he turned to Carter, recovered a more subdued version of his usual jovial self and gave him a weak smile. "I might want to try that stand-up thing. So, you, ah… You want to sit behind this desk?"

Carter looked to his designers and Pearl, and nodded. "Yeah, I do."

"Alright-y then," Harry said, giving his suspenders a snap. "It's yours." He reached out and patted Carter on the shoulder. "You've done good, nephew. Better than me. But I do have one condition."

"What's that?"

Harry strode across the room and reached into the glass cabinet. "I take my clown head with me." As he grabbed the toy out of the cabinet and walked out of the room, the plastic head chortled.

Daphne watched the man and his clown leave Carter's office, before she entered the room. She paused a moment in the doorway, watching him talk to another man who sat across from him. Carter's tie was a little askew, his hair a little mussed. He looked sexy and vulnerable, all at the same time. She thought of the check in her purse, the ring on her finger, and something in Daphne's chest constricted. "Carter?"

He looked over, a smile washing over his features when their gazes connected.

"Daphne." She felt his name roll off her tongue, nearly a caress.

He gestured toward the man, an older version of himself. "Come in. I'd like you to meet my father."

The introductions were completed, then Jonathon Matthews gave his son a short, quick nod. "I'll be on my way." He rose, crossed to the door, then paused and toed at the floor, as if he'd found a piece of lint. "I'd, ah, like it if the two of you were my guests for dinner tonight."

"That'd be great, Dad," Carter said. "Really great." His father nodded, then left, shutting the door as he did.

They were alone. Tension sizzled between them, even with six feet of distance separating their bodies. Carter rose, skirted his desk and came to stand before her. "I didn't expect to see you today."

"I didn't expect to be here." She watched his eyes, those deep, dark blue eyes, which reflected a different Carter Matthews from the picture painted by the gossip columns. This man, the one she knew, had multiple facets that went beyond the fast car and the playboy charm.

But he was also a man who was asking something of her that she wasn't sure she could give.

She had paced her apartment for a long while today, then gone with Kim to retrieve Daphne's car, all the while trying to decide whether to run to or run away from her hasty decision. The emotions that had been tumbling inside her in the last few days, making her wonder if maybe it was possible to have it all—the job, the guy, the life. That sometimes choices made on the fly could work out in the end.

She reached into her bag and pulled out the small green army man that had fallen on the floor a few days earlier. "Tell me why this upset you so much," she said, needing to know what made this man tick. And why every beat of his heart seemed to connect with hers.

He took the toy in his hand, turning it over in his palm, the tiny point of the rifle making little red indents in his skin. "When my mother walked out on our family, Cade and I were in the yard. Playing army men. Being boys. She stopped by the sandbox, gave us a kiss, then climbed in the car and never looked back." He closed his grip over the toy and inhaled a long, tight breath. Daphne reached out for him, a hand on his arm, giving him the time, the space, he needed to finish. "That was the last time I can remember really playing. Having fun. Everything changed after that, especially our father. Cade and I had to grow up very fast." He paused a moment, then the trademark Carter grin was back. "Well, *Cade* grew up fast. I took a little longer."

Sympathy shimmered in Daphne. She knew that kind of life; understood the man he had become, and why he'd done it. "Me, too. Having to grow up so fast made me…" She paused, searching for the words. "Afraid of anything that might come close to chaos. I picked men who were boring. Lived a life that was so predictable, I was sleepwalking through it." A smile curved across her face. "Then I met you."

"And I turned your life upside-down," he said. "Just as you did mine."

"Maybe you can handle that, Carter, but I…" Her voice trailed off, suddenly unable to voice those final words. It had to be that he was standing so close, watching her so intently, that every glance seemed to read into her soul. "I can't."

"We were both abandoned, Daphne." Carter took her hands, his grip warm and secure. The kind she could fall into as easy as a blink. "Don't you think that affects how we view relationships?"

"Maybe," she said, then paused and drew in a breath, and dug into that well of honesty that had been waiting for her to face her past, face herself. "Okay, yes."

"And you're worried that you repeated history when we eloped."

"I did," Daphne said. "I did exactly what my mother always did. Married a man just because he asked me."

Carter took a step forward, capturing her jaw with his hand. "Is that the only reason you married me?"

She leaned into his touch, craving it as much as she knew she should push it away. Something had happened between her and Carter Matthews in the last few days, something powerful and terrifying.

And wonderful.

"No," she breathed, knowing now as she stood here, there was no way she could walk away from this man. Couldn't say goodbye. Couldn't say marrying him had been a huge mistake.

Because she had fallen in love with Carter Matthews.

Carter brushed back a tendril of hair, a touch so gentle, so soft, she wanted to cry. "I didn't marry you to repair my reputation or to get out of paying the bill for the retreat." That grin again. "I married you, Daphne Williams-Matthews, because I love you."

The words exploded inside her in a burst of new, bright hues of unexpected emotions and revelations.

Carter loved her.

Did it matter if he'd fallen in love with her over the course of days or over the course of years? Did it matter if it took her a moment to know he was the one—or a lifetime?

And what a mistake would it be, if she took too long and then lost all that could have been? What if hesitating cost her the very thing she wanted?

Because she already had it right here. Five days ago, her heart hadn't followed the rules of her brain; it had gone and followed his. "I love you, too," she said.

A smile took over his face, lighting his eyes. Disbelief gave way to joy and he leaned down, kissing her with sweet tenderness. "You had me worried there," he said.

"It's good to keep you on your toes." She cupped his face, hearing their words sing inside her. "You certainly did that with me when you left that check."

"I believe in you, Daphne. I believe in what you're doing. And when you get that creativity center built, sign me up for the Crayolas."

She laughed. "You want to get in there and do some coloring?"

He nodded, and the tease momentarily left his eyes. "I think doing that is long overdue. I'd like to have some fun in my life."

"I thought that's all playboys did," she said, teasing him, but thrilled inside to have a man who loved her and loved her work. And this man in particular.

"Driving a fast car and going eighteen holes is nothing compared to the fun I know I'm going to have with you." He touched her lips, a light, soft touch that whispered the words in his heart. Anticipation fired inside her. "You know, I think we need to go back to Maine."

Her brow wrinkled. "Why?"

He grinned. "Because you're not the only one with creative thinking. I have a few lessons I'd like to teach you." He leaned down and whispered in her ear, giving her a hot preview of what would be coming in the days ahead.

"Oh, Carter," she said, laughing and already fantasizing. "I'm not sure the ping-pong table is strong enough for *that*."

"But we'll have a hell of a lot of fun finding out what's going to happen, won't we?"

Daphne looked into the eyes of her husband and thought of the years ahead, the fun that was just beginning. "Yes, I believe we will."

Then she kissed him, the two of them both winning at the best game of all. Love.

* * * * *

THE ROYAL HOUSE OF NIROLI
Always passionate, always proud

The richest royal family in the world—
united by blood and passion,
torn apart by deceit and desire

Nestled in the azure blue of the Mediterranean Sea, the majestic island of Niroli has prospered for centuries. The Fierezza men have worn the crown with passion and pride since ancient times. But now, as the king's health declines, and his two sons have been tragically killed, the crown is in jeopardy.

The clock is ticking—a new heir must be found before the king is forced to abdicate. By royal decree the internationally scattered members of the Fierezza family are summoned to claim their destiny. But any person who takes the throne must do so according to The Rules of the Royal House of Niroli. Soon secrets and rivalries emerge as the descendents of this ancient royal line vie for position and power. Only a true Fierezza can become ruler—a person dedicated to their country, their people…and their eternal love!

Each month starting in July 2007,
Harlequin Presents is delighted to bring you
an exciting installment from
THE ROYAL HOUSE OF NIROLI,
in which you can follow the epic search
for the true Nirolian king.
Eight heirs, eight romances, eight fantastic stories!

Here's your chance to enjoy a sneak preview of the first book delivered to you by royal decree…

FIVE minutes later she was standing immobile in front of the study's window, her original purpose of coming in forgotten, as she stared in shocked horror at the envelope she was holding. Waves of heat followed by icy chill surged through her body. She could hardly see the address now through her blurred vision, but the crest on its left-hand front corner stood out, its *royal* crest, followed by the address: *HRH Prince Marco of Niroli...*

She didn't hear Marco's key in the apartment door, she didn't even hear him calling out her name. Her shock was so great that nothing could penetrate it. It encased her in a kind of bubble, which only concentrated the torment of what she was suffering and branded it on her brain so that it could never be forgotten. It was only finally pierced by the sudden opening of the study door as Marco walked in.

"Welcome home, *Your Highness*. I suppose I ought to curtsy." She waited, praying that he would laugh and tell her that she had got it all wrong, that the envelope she was holding, addressing him as Prince Marco of Niroli, was some silly mistake. But like a tiny candle flame shivering vulnerably in the dark, her hope trembled fearfully. And then the look in Marco's eyes extinguished it as cruelly as a hand placed callously over a dying person's face to stem their last breath.

"Give that to me," he demanded, taking the envelope from her.

"It's too late, Marco," Emily told him brokenly. "I know the truth now…." She dug her teeth in her lower lip to try to force back her own pain.

"You had no right to go through my desk," Marco shot back at her furiously, full of loathing at being caught off-guard and forced into a position in which he was in the wrong, making him determined to find something he could accuse Emily of. "I trusted you…."

Emily could hardly believe what she was hearing. "No, you didn't trust me, Marco, and you didn't trust me because you knew that I couldn't trust you. And you knew that because you're a liar, and liars don't trust people because they know that they themselves cannot be trusted." She not only felt sick, she also felt as though she could hardly breathe. "You are Prince Marco of Niroli…. How could you not tell me who you are and still live with me as intimately as we have lived together?" she demanded brokenly.

"Stop being so ridiculously dramatic," Marco demanded fiercely. "You are making too much of the situation."

"*Too much?*" Emily almost screamed the words at him. "When were you going to tell me, Marco? Perhaps you just planned to walk away without telling me anything? After all, what do my feelings matter to you?"

"Of course they matter." Marco stopped her sharply. "And it was in part to protect them, and you, that I decided not to inform you when my grandfather first announced that he intended to step down from the throne and hand it on to me."

"To protect me?" Emily nearly choked on her fury. "Hand on the throne? No wonder you told me when you first took me to bed that all you wanted was sex. You *knew* that was the only kind of relationship there could ever be between us! You *knew* that one day you would be Niroli's king. No doubt you are expected to marry a princess. Is she picked out for you already, your *royal* bride?"

* * * * *

Look for
THE FUTURE KING'S PREGNANT
MISTRESS
by Penny Jordan in July 2007,
from Harlequin Presents,
available wherever books are sold.

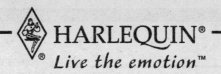

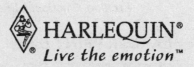

HARLEQUIN®
INTRIGUE®

BREATHTAKING ROMANTIC SUSPENSE

Shared dangers and passions lead to electrifying
romance and heart-stopping suspense!

Every month, you'll meet six new heroes
who are guaranteed to make your spine tingle
and your pulse pound. With them you'll enter
into the exciting world of Harlequin Intrigue—
where your life is on the line
and so is your heart!

THAT'S INTRIGUE—
ROMANTIC SUSPENSE
AT ITS BEST!

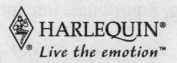

HARLEQUIN®
Live the emotion™

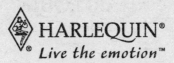

Harlequin® Historical
Historical Romantic Adventure!

*Imagine a time of chivalrous
knights and unconventional ladies,
roguish rakes and impetuous
heiresses, rugged cowboys
and spirited frontierswomen—
these rich and vivid tales will
capture your imagination!*

*Harlequin Historical . . .
they're too good to miss!*

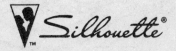